Chris heard it first, calling it up from some deep, recessed memory of his days in the Gulf War. It sounded rather like an empty freight car rolling down a railroad track.

"Incoming!" he shouted, diving for the ground.

None of the others actually recognized the sound, since none of them had ever been exposed to it, but they knew how to react first and ask questions later, so they dived to the ground as soon as Chris did.

The arcing sound continued for another few seconds, then there was an explosion in one of the small, family quarters.

Almost right on top of that came several more arcing sounds, followed quickly by explosions.

"Son of a bitch! They're using artillery on us!" Chris said.

The next thing they heard was the low growl of helicopter engines. They could hear them but not see them. Then, popping up just over the tree line, were two Bell Jet Rangers. They were firing rockets into the camp, and as people ran across the camp parade ground, they were cut down by machine-gun fire from the helicopters.

When the helicopters pulled up from their firing run, John got a good look at them. They were painted olive drab, and on the tail cone was a white ball inside an orange circle. Inside the white ball was a black, four-corner star.

BOOK YOUR PLACE ON OUR WEBSITE AND MAKE THE READING CONNECTION!

We've created a customized website just for our very special readers, where you can get the inside scoop on everything that's going on with Zebra, Pinnacle and Kensington books.

When you come online, you'll have the exciting opportunity to:

- View covers of upcoming books
- Read sample chapters
- Learn about our future publishing schedule (listed by publication month *and author*)
- Find out when your favorite authors will be visiting a city near you
- Search for and order backlist books from our online catalog
- Check out author bios and background information
- Send e-mail to your favorite authors
- Meet the Kensington staff online
- Join us in weekly chats with authors, readers and other guests
- Get writing guidelines
- AND MUCH MORE!

Visit our website at
http://www.kensingtonbooks.com

WILLIAM W. JOHNSTONE

CODE NAME: KILL ZONE

PINNACLE BOOKS
Kensington Publishing Corp.
http://www.kensingtonbooks.com

PINNACLE BOOKS are published by

Kensington Publishing Corp.
850 Third Avenue
New York, NY 10022

All Kensington Titles, Imprints and Distributed Lines are
available at special quantity discounts for bulk purchases for
sales promotion, premiums, fund-raising, and educational or
institutional use. Special book excerpts or customized print-
ings can also be created to fit specific needs. For details,
write or phone the office of the Kensington special sales
manager: Kensington Publishing Corp., 850 Third Avenue,
New York, NY 10022, attn: Special Sales Department,
Phone: 1-800-221-2647.

Pinnacle and the P logo Reg. U.S. Pat. & TM Off.

First Pinnacle Books Printing: May 2005

10 9 8 7 6 5 4 3 2 1

Printed in the United States of America

Chapter 1

Cali, Colombia

Katy Correal stood at the windows, looking outside. There was about her a subtle suggestion of Toujours Moi perfume . . . the fragrance notes of
sandalwood and vetiver, with a floral touch and
musky undertones. A soft breeze lifted the lace curtain so that it fluttered about her naked body. The
diaphanous screen accented rather than concealed
the curves and shadows. Brian Skipper was also
nude, and he lay on the bed in his small, one-room
apartment, enjoying the view thus displayed.

The morning light splashed through the window,
causing Katy's skin to take on a golden glow. Brian was
sure he had never seen anyone so beautiful.

Katy had spent the night with him last night.

"Hey," he said.

Katy turned her head toward him, pushing the
curtain out of the way as she did so.

"Why such a serious expression?" Brian asked. "You
look like someone stole your candy. Give me a smile."

Katy smiled.

"That's more like it."

Katy raised her hand to brush her hair back from
her face. As she did so, it caused her right breast to

flatten somewhat, but that just added to her overall sensuality.

"When are you going to come live with me?" he asked.

Katy shook her head no, but she said nothing.

"Come on, what's the big deal? Last night was the third time this week you spent the night with me. And you've been averaging two or three nights a week for a month now."

"It would not be right to come live with you," she said.

"Why not?"

"My employers would not approve."

"Do you think the Ministry of Agriculture would approve of all the times you have slept with me?"

Again, Katy shook her head no.

"Then what's the difference between sleeping with me and living with me?"

"It is different."

Brian sighed and shook his head. "Well, if there is a difference, I sure can't see it."

"You will go back to America soon. And when you do, you will forget me."

"Oh, darlin', I don't think I can ever forget you," Brian said. "And who knows? I might come back someday."

"When?"

"Oh, I don't know. Maybe I'll come back when your farmers need me again."

"Maybe you can quit your job and stay here," Katy suggested.

Brian shook his head. "And what would I do if I stayed here?"

"The same thing I do. Work for the *Ministerio de Agricultura y Desarrollo.*"

"Darlin', I can barely stand all the red tape and

horseshit in Washington. There's no way I'm going to replace one bureaucracy with another."

Katy came back to the bed, then sat beside him. Leaning toward him, she smiled at him seductively and put her hand on his chest. Brian couldn't help but wonder how her cool fingers could give off such heat.

"You could farm," she said.

"Farm?" Brian chuckled. "That's a good one. How am I going to farm? I don't know anything about farming."

Katy's eyes opened wider in surprise. "Why do you say you know nothing about farming? You are an adviser for the U.S. Department of Agriculture. You must know much about farming."

Brian laughed, then reached up to let his own fingers linger on the pearlike curve of her breast.

"Darlin', I'm what you call an expert," he said. "An expert is someone who tells other people how to do things. That doesn't mean he can do them himself."

Katy laughed. "You are funny," she said. "You should be a . . . how do you say . . . *cómico artístico?*"

"Stand-up comedian," Brian said.

"*Sí.* You should be a stand-up comedian."

Brian's fingers followed the curve of her breast until they reached the nipple. There, he kneaded the little button of flesh and it grew hard and responsive.

"Believe me, honey, right now a stand-up comedian is the last thing I want to be," he said.

"What do you want?" she asked. She leaned over him then, and her long raven hair fell forward until he could feel its softness caressing his chest. She trailed her hand down his chest and across his stomach, then she wrapped her long, cool fingers around him.

"Oh yeah. You know what I want," Brian said, his voice thick now, with need.

"*Sí*, I know what you want," Katy said, now gently stroking him as she leaned over to kiss him. "I will give you what you want." Her words were lost in his mouth.

Two hours later

The speeding jeep turned left so sharply off Calle 15 onto Carrera 3 that it lifted up on two wheels, and it was only the skill of the driver that prevented the vehicle from turning over.

One of the two drivers chasing him did not make the turn and, trying desperately to follow him, jerked the wheel around. As a result the Mercedes flipped over, rolled several times, then caught fire. Several bystanders started toward the flaming vehicle with the intent to help the occupants, but turned and ran when the ammunition in the burning car started cooking off, sending bullets whizzing and screaming in all directions.

The second pursuing Mercedes made the turn, and from the passenger side a man stuck his head and shoulders through the open window and fired at the fleeing jeep. The driver of the jeep heard the bullets whistle by him, then saw them crash through the windshield in front of him.

He made another abrupt turn onto Calle 12, then slid to a halt in front of the gate of the American consulate. Because he was at the consulate, the pursuing car went on by. The Colombian gatekeeper stepped out of the guardhouse.

"Senor?" he said.

"Where's Camilo?"

"Camilo is sick."

"I'm Brian Skipper with the U.S. State Department," Brian said, flashing his ID. "Open the gate."

"*Sí*, senor," the guard said. He stepped back into the guardhouse and as he did, Brian glanced down the street where he saw the Mercedes that had been chasing him. It was stopped now, and the driver and his passenger were out of the car, looking back toward him.

"Better luck next time, assholes!" Brian shouted, laughing and flipping them the finger.

With Brian's attention directed toward the Mercedes, he did not notice Camilo lying dead on the gatehouse floor, and he did not see the guard lifting his Uzi.

"What's keeping you with this gate?" Brian asked, turning back toward the gate guard. It wasn't until then that he saw the Uzi pointed at him.

Brian wasted no time in asking questions. Instead, he went for his own gun and actually managed to clear his holster before the guard opened fire. The guard emptied an entire clip at Brian, hitting him in the chest, head, and neck. Blood and brain detritus flew from his head as Brian fell back across the gearshift lever.

The Mercedes that had been waiting now did a squealing U-turn in the street, came back up to the consulate gate, and stopped just long enough for the guard to jump in. The car left, its rear tires squealing and burning rubber as it peeled away.

CIA Headquarters, Langley, Virginia

Harley Thomas sat at his computer, studying the file on the screen. There was a photograph of Brian

Skipper, along with a descriptive paragraph. He put the cursor over the word *Reports* and clicked the mouse.

ENTRY FOR AUTHORIZED PERSONNEL ONLY. ENTER USER NAME AND PASSWORD.

Harley typed in his name, then the password, and opened the file.

> *There is a possibility, though I believe it to be remote, that my cover as an agricultural consultant may have been compromised. I have a meeting tomorrow with a local operative who can substantiate the last report I submitted. I will submit the results of that meeting as soon as possible.*

Harley scrolled back through the previous reports. If these reports were accurate, then the U.S. would soon have a major problem to contend with. And to make matters worse, there were no government assets to deal with the problem.

Harley closed the file, then picked up the phone and called the deputy director.

"I've been going over Brian Skipper's reports," he said, when he got the deputy director on the phone.

"And?" the DD replied.

Harley sighed. "And I think the information is valid."

"Damn."

"I have a suggestion."

"And what would that be?"

"I think we should outsource the job."

"Outsource? You mean turn it over to another agency?"

"No, there is no government agency that can handle this problem. When I say outsource, I mean really outsource. Beyond the government."

"You aren't talking offshore, are you?"

"No, this won't involve a foreign government. It will be local talent."

There was a long pause at the other end of the line. Then the deputy director spoke. "You do know, don't you, that we will not be able to fund this? Every penny we spend is under such intense scrutiny that it is impossible to hide anything."

"We won't need to fund it."

"Wait a minute, are you telling me that you can get this handled without it costing us anything?"

"Yes."

"Harley . . . " the deputy director started, but he stopped.

"Yes?"

The DD sighed. "Can you put up enough firewalls to protect us?"

"By us, do you mean protect the agency from governmental oversight, or protect the government from the press and foreign concern?"

"All of the above."

"Yes, I can do that."

"This conversation never took place."

"What conversation?"

Chapter 2

The Code Name Team was in residence at their headquarters, a sprawling house in the desert of southwest Texas. The Code Name Team was an extralegal, rather than illegal, group whose job it was to "handle" things that fell through the cracks of legal technicality. The team was created to take care of those dregs of society, the terrorists, murderers, drug dealers, etc., who too often got away with their misdeeds because of misguided liberal guilt over the normal inequities of nature.

The Code Name Team had no connection with the government. Instead, it was funded by a consortium of very wealthy people, mostly Americans, but some foreigners, who had a highly developed sense of right and wrong. There were, however, a few highly placed individuals in the government who knew about them, and privately appreciated what the team was doing. But knowledge of the Code Name Team's existence was kept on such a need-to-know basis that it was cellular in structure. Those who did know about it had no idea who else knew about it.

Because of the supersecret nature of the team, its members had no family or social life. They had no future and they had burned all the bridges to their past. There was more than one way into the team, but there was only one way out, and that was in a body bag. The men and women of the Code Name Team were teammates, coworkers, fellow warriors, friends, and family, in and of themselves.

Those few times they were able to come together without a specific assignment were rare, and when they did, they managed to find ways to unwind and relax.

As several sides of pork ribs were barbecuing over a mesquite fire, the members of the team were spread out around the residence. Some were out on the patio, kicked back and drinking beer. Mike Rojas was reading a paperback western. Mike was Mexican-American, and though his family had maintained its Mexican heritage, he was quick to point out that he had an ancestor who was at the Alamo, fighting on the side of the Americans.

Mike was like Sylvester Stallone, rather short, but powerfully built. When his enthusiastic pursuit of tax cheaters made enemies in high places, he decided it was time to leave government service.

Chris Farmer was kneeling on the ground in front of a disassembled weapon. Blindfolded, he was re-assembling it. Chris qualified for the 1984 Olympics in the shooting competition, and his qualifying score was enough to have won him a gold medal. But in an unprecedented move, President Carter used the Olympics as a means of lodging a political protest against the Soviets, and Chris did not get to go. Born and raised a Democrat, Chris turned Republican that year.

His natural shooting talent did not go unnoticed, however, and he became a trained army sniper who, during the first Gulf War, compiled a record of seventeen confirmed kills, not one from closer than one thousand yards.

Jennifer Barnes and Linda Marsh were watching him.

Jennifer was a former FBI agent. At five feet four inches, she was rather small, but she liked to say that dynamite came in small packages. She could say that, literally, because she was the team's explosives expert who could, in her words, "make a bomb from shit and sugar." With her blond hair, blue eyes, and perfect shape, Jennifer could turn the head of any man.

Linda Marsh was the real beauty though, dark-haired and sultry, with a very voluptuous figure. Her golden skin tone sometimes left a person wondering just what racial blending created such a beautiful package. That often worked to her advantage, enabling her to pass herself off as any race she wished.

A former member of the Los Angeles Police Department, Linda was an accomplished martial artist.

"Only a real gun nut would pass the time by disassembling and reassembling his gun," Jennifer said.

"It's not a gun!" Chris barked. "It's a weapon, a rifle, a piece."

"No," Paul Brewer said. "That is a gun, Linda is a piece."

"You wish, asshole," Linda said, laughing.

Paul was a forty-year-old black man who had spent fifteen years with the border patrol. An All-American football player at Ohio State, Paul also played for five years in the Canadian Football League.

The team leader, John Barrone, was inside the house standing at the window, looking out at the others as they relaxed on the patio. John spent twenty-two years with the CIA before leaving to become the field commander of the Code Name

Team. He was fifty-one years old, average size and build, but in excellent physical shape.

John had never remarried since the death of his wife, Michelle, though he would be considered a very good catch. He was from "the New England Barrones," an exceptionally wealthy family whose tax returns were gone over very carefully.

Wagner handed him a note and John read it, closed his eyes for a moment, and shook his head. He sighed.

"Is it confirmed?" John asked.

"I'm sorry, yes, it is," Wagner said. "Don Yee just took it off the computer."

Wagner had no field operational experience and never went on a mission, but he was the titular head of the group because he was the contact between the Code Name Team and their sponsors. He also had important contacts within the government.

"How well did you know him?" Wagner asked.

"Brian Skipper?" John sighed. "We were pretty close. He was best man at my wedding."

"That is close," Wagner said. "I'm sorry, John. I truly am."

"Do we know what happened?"

"Only that he was shot outside the gates of the American consulate in Cali."

"A drive-by?"

"Well, if it was a drive-by, it was a drive-by shooting and stripping," Wagner said.

"What do you mean?"

"The gate guard was also dead. They found him lying in the floor of the gatehouse, dressed only in his underwear."

"Damn, that means Brian was set up," John said. "Someone killed the guard, took his clothes, and posed as the guard. When Brian showed up, he shot him."

"Sounds like it to me," Wagner said. "Though the news reports are treating it as a random shooting."

Don Yee came into the den from the computer room. Don Yee was the resident computer geek and communications expert. He could hack into any system, anywhere. He was Chinese, but one of his ancestors jumped ship in New York in 1830, and Don's family had been American ever since.

"John, there is a call for you on the scrambler," Don said.

"Thanks," John said. He followed Don back into the computer room, then picked up the special phone.

"This is Barrone," he said.

"John, this is Harley Thomas."

"Harley, I haven't heard from you in a while," John said. "What can I do for you?"

Harley had been the last partner John had worked with before he left the CIA.

"You can come to Washington, that's what you can do for me."

"When?"

"As soon as you can get here. We need to talk."

"Can you give me a hint? We are scrambled, you know."

"Yes, it's about Brian Skipper. His killing wasn't a random act. He was on to something. Something big."

"I'm on my way," John said.

Washington, D.C.

John was in his suite at the St. Gregory Hotel in Washington when he heard a light knock on his door. Glancing through the peephole, he saw Harley Thomas standing in the hall. He opened the door.

"Hello, Harley," he said, stepping back to allow Harley entry.

"John," Harley answered. Coming into the room, he stepped quickly over to the window, then looked down toward the parking lot. After that, he took out a small handheld device and swept it around the room.

"There are no bugs," John said. "I've already swept the room."

"Have you left the room for any reason? To get a Coke? Newspaper?"

"No," John answered.

Satisfied that the room was clean, Harley breathed a sigh of relief, then walked over to sit on the sofa.

"Looks like I taught you well," John said, chuckling.

"Don't think I don't remember," Harley replied. "I've used your 'John's practical class to save your ass' a lot of times since then. And I've passed it on to a lot of newbies over the years."

"I made some coffee," John said, crossing over to the service counter next to the TV. "Would you like a cup?"

"Yes, thanks. Black."

John poured two cups of coffee, then handed one to Harley.

"Have you ever heard of Pangea?" Harley asked as he took the cup.

"Pangea? Yes. Isn't that what scientists call the giant continent, back before the continents drifted apart to form Europe, the Americas, and so forth?"

"Yes," Harley said. "But that's not the Pangea I'm talking about."

"Well then, I'll just have to shut up and listen,"

John said. "Because that's the only Pangea I've ever heard of."

"You'll hear about this one soon enough," Harley said. "Everyone will."

"Let me guess. Pangea has something to do with what Brian was working on. And, since he was in Cali, then I'm going to guess that it has something to do with dope."

"It does," Harley said. "At fifty-two billion dollars per year, the drug cartel based in Cali, Colombia, is the largest player in the multibillion-dollar world-wide cocaine industry. The head of it is a man named Luiz Mendoza."

"Yes, I've heard of him. But shouldn't that be a DEA problem? What was Brian doing down there? He's with the CIA. Unless he changed agencies."

"No, Brian was still with the CIA. That's where the sovereign nation of Pangea comes in."

"You just lost me with that one," John said. "What sovereign nation of Pangea?"

"Well, there is no such thing as the sovereign nation of Pangea."

"I didn't think so."

"But there soon will be, if Mendoza has his way."

"Oh?"

"Mendoza has decided to secede from Colombia," Harley said. "He has drawn a line on the map, from the coast just north of Medellin, down to and including Florencia, then straight down to the border with Peru. If he succeeds, everything inside that line, and that includes Quibdo, Pereira, Armenia, Cali, Florencia, Mocoa, Pasto, and Popayán, would belong to the new nation of Pangea. And it should come as no surprise that he has established himself as *el presidente* for life."

"So, he's declared civil war against Colombia and Colombia is asking the U.S. for help, right?"

Harley shook his head. "No. I wish it was as easy as a simple civil war."

"Wait a minute. You wish it was as *easy* as a civil war?" John replied, surprised by Harley's comment.

"Yes. Then it would be a matter for our State Department and the Department of Defense."

"I don't understand. How does he plan to set up an entirely new country without a revolution?"

"He has bought it."

"What?"

"He has paid off enough politicians in Bogata that they have sold out. Our people tell us that Mendoza now has enough votes in the Colombian Congress to give him what he is asking for, and sixty days from now the government in Bogata will vote to give them their independence. As soon as that happens, Pangea will seek international recognition."

"Do you think they will get it? International recognition, I mean."

"France has already agreed to be their sponsor for membership in the United Nations."

"Yeah," John said. "Well, they would, wouldn't they?"

"You can see the problem that causes us," Harley said. "If Pangea becomes an independent nation, its principal . . . practically its only export will be dope. That will put a serious crimp in our drug war. At least now we have some cooperation with the Colombian Government. Pangea would be the first nation in history to have its official GNP based upon the exporting of drugs. And who do you think their biggest customer will be?"

"The U.S.," John said.

"Precisely. And once Pangea attains recognition,

our hands are tied. It will be a sovereign nation and we won't be able to act against them militarily without violating international law. And we can't negotiate with them diplomatically because we have no intention of granting them recognition."

"That leaves?" John said.

"You. You and your team."

John nodded. "Yeah, I thought you might be getting around to that."

"You are our only hope," Harley said. "For reasons that I have already expressed, we can't act militarily. And we can't put in CIA or DEA operatives. That leaves you."

John drummed his fingers on the arm of the chair for a few moments.

"What, exactly, would you have us do?"

"I've outlined the problem for you," Harley said.

"Yes."

"I want you to do whatever it takes to make the problem go away."

"Whatever it takes?"

"Yes."

"No restrictions of any kind?"

Harley held up his hands. "The United States Government can't put any restrictions on you, because, officially, we don't even know that you exist. And if any of your team gets caught, we won't lift a finger to help you."

"I see."

"I'm not sure that you do see," Harley said. "Because when I say we won't lift a finger, I mean just that. From the moment you leave this hotel room, you are absolutely on your own. You will get no help of any kind from us. Do not try to contact us, do not expect us to contact you. As far as we are concerned, you do not exist."

"Yeah, I know, we've been down this path before."

"Well, there is one thing that is different this time," Harley said. He smiled. "You might call it an incentive of sorts."

"What is that?"

"Mendoza has an off-the-records cash reserve of five hundred million dollars."

"Half a billion dollars?"

"Yes."

"That's interesting."

"I thought that might get your attention. And since we are disavowing anything to do with you, the U.S. Government has no interest in that money."

"That means?"

"That means that the five hundred million dollars is yours, if you can get it."

"Well, as you said, that is an incentive of sorts."

"Oh, one more thing."

"Yes?"

"Katy Correal."

"What about Katy Correal?"

"She works for the Colombian Agricultural Ministry, and was Brian's contact with that agency."

John looked confused. "What would Brian have to do with the agricultural industry?"

"His cover was that of an agricultural consultant," Harley explained.

"I see. Did this woman, Katy, know what his real purpose was?"

Harley shook his head. "Not exactly, though one of his mandates was to locate the coca farms. And I'm sure she was aware of that."

"Is there a problem with her?"

"We're not sure. But we do know that the relationship had gone a little beyond her being his contact with the agricultural ministry."

"By beyond, you mean he was sleeping with her."

Harley nodded.

"How do you know? Did Brian say that?"

"No. But we did have some independent observation that—"

"Wait a minute. You had a tail on Brian?"

"A backup, for his own safety," Harley said, quickly. "Come on, John, you know how these things work."

"Yeah, I know," John said. "Sorry, I didn't mean anything by it."

"Anyway, the backup reported that Katy was a regular visitor to Brian's apartment, arriving at night and not leaving until the next morning."

"Yes, well, I can see where he might get the idea that Brian was sleeping with her," John said. "But he's divorced, or rather, was divorced. So I figure that what he did was his own business."

"I agree," Harley said. "I just brought it up as additional, call it useless, information."

"So noted."

"Remember, John, after this, no more contact between us for the duration of this operation. Not for anything. You are one hundred percent on your own."

"I never heard of you," John replied.

Harley put his cup down, stood up, and walked over to the door. He paused there for just a second, as if he were going to say one more word, but he said nothing. Without looking back, without so much as a good-bye, he laid a manila envelope on the table by the door, then left.

John waited a moment, then called the front desk.

"Get a limousine for me, would you? I'm checking out."

"You are checking out? But, Mr. Barrone, according to our records you only arrived one hour ago. Is your room unsatisfactory."

"The room is fine," John said. "But I've had a change of plans."

"Very good, sir, I'll get the limo for you."

Half an hour later, John was on the way to Dulles International. Through the window he watched a 767 on final, then he realized that he hadn't made any arrangements to get back to the compound from DFW. He dialed a number on his cell phone.

"This is John," he said. "Tell Don to meet me at DFW. My flight arrives at five-nineteen."

Chapter 3

After John selected the team that would be accompanying him, they gathered in the den for a briefing. He held up the manila envelope that Harley had left in his room.

"Operation Rolling Thunder," John said.

"Rolling Thunder, good name," Mike said. "My older brother was an Air Force pilot in Vietnam. Operation Rolling Thunder was what they called the bombing raids, early in the war."

"Your brother was shot down then, wasn't he?" Paul asked.

Mike nodded. "Yes. He's still MIA."

"I'm sorry."

"Rolling Thunder. I'll dedicate this operation to him," Mike said.

"We all will," John said.

"Hear! Hear!" Chris replied.

"Okay, to get on with the briefing," John said. He took a sheet of paper from the manila folder. "This is a list of our friends and enemies. Only there is a caveat."

"What sort of caveat?" Jennifer asked.

"The degree of confidence is only seventy percent," John said. "That means if we contact ten friends, three of them are likely to be enemies."

"That's not very reassuring," Linda said.

"I know, but it's a start. Wagner, you wanted to say a few words?" John invited.

"Yes," Wagner said. He stood to face the others. "First, let me tell you that I wish I could go with you."

"You can take my place, Mr. Wagner," Mike said.

"No, no, that's quite all right, I, uh, wouldn't want to deprive you of your fun," Wagner replied. The others laughed because, though Wagner always said he wished he could go, all knew that he didn't actually want to go at all.

No one thought any less of him for it. They knew that what they did was considerably beyond normal.

"Before your departure you will be issued rather substantial funds."

"Hey, how about we take a shortcut through Vegas?" Jennifer suggested.

"Oh, I think not," Wagner replied stiffly.

"Well, you don't have to be so tight-assed about it," Mike said, and the others laughed.

"May we please continue with the briefing?" Wagner asked.

"We're all ears," Chris said. "Well, Mike is, anyway," he added, alluding to Mike's rather large ears.

Again, everyone laughed.

John saw that Wagner was beginning to get a little frustrated, but he made no effort to stop the banter. He knew what he would be asking of the team, and he knew that when it came right down to it, he would be able to put his life in their hands. If they wanted to be a little loose right now, they had earned that right, many times over.

"One final thing before I take your questions," Wagner said. "We will be operating on the terminal-response countersign system. So, know your passwords."

There was a moment of silence as everyone absorbed what Wagner had just told them. Terminal response was serious stuff. That meant that when you gave the password, or were challenged with the password, there had better be an exact and immediate response. The wrong response, or even a hesitation in the response, would require the challenger to kill the person who did not respond.

"Any questions?" Wagner asked.

"Yeah, what about weapons?" Chris asked.

"John, you want to handle that one?" Wagner asked.

John stood up again. "We think we have a source. If our information is right, we'll get them as soon as we arrive," he said.

"And if it's not right?" Chris asked.

"We'll get them as soon as we arrive," John said again.

Chris nodded. "All right," he replied. "I can live with that."

Wagner looked over at Don. "Don, do you have your report ready for us?"

Don was eating a sandwich, and he poked a dangling piece of ham into his mouth, then chewed furiously to get it all down before he spoke.

"I've run a computer search and analysis on some of the key personnel on our friends list," he said. "This is what I found."

"Archbishop Quintero Duarte, seventy-two, is the archbishop of Cali. He studied at Georgetown University here in America, and speaks excellent English. Ten years ago he was kidnapped by the FARC, the so-called Revolutionary Forces of Colombia. They demanded a ransom of one million dollars from the Catholic Church, but Duarte escaped, foiling their plans. He is an outspoken opponent of the Pangean secession. He appears to be the genuine thing.

"Viktor Marin runs a bicycle shop in Cali. He is a former police lieutenant who was kicked off the force for engaging in graft."

"Wow, a Colombian police officer engaging in graft is like a Colombian police officer speaking Spanish," Mike said, and the others laughed.

"You say he runs a bicycle shop?" Linda asked.

Don nodded. "Yes, and he really does sell and repair bicycles. But that's just a front for his main business, which is arms dealing. But not just arms, you can get anything you want from Viktor Marin: weapons, ammunition, vehicles, forged documents. He launders money and has been known to move drugs."

"And he's one of our 'good' guys?" Chris asked.

"Not exactly," Don replied. "He's anyone's man who has the money to pay him."

"Come on, you don't expect us to use someone like that, do you?" Mike asked.

"I'm just reading the reports," Don said. "I didn't select these people."

"Look, we'll need a source of supply once we are down there, and he's the only game in town," John explained. "Anyway, there's something to be said for knowing the devil you are dealing with. The best way to handle him is to always be on the alert."

"Yeah, I guess you're right," Mike agreed.

"Go ahead, Don," John said.

"The next two are Ricardo and Esteban Cortina."

"Brothers? Father and son?" Chris asked.

Don shook his head. "Ricardo is Esteban's uncle. Ricardo is a former general in the Colombian Army, and distinguished himself in many battles with the FARC. In that, he was following in the footsteps of his father, Manuel Cortina, who was a general under President Eduardo Santos, during World War Two."

"World War Two? What did Colombia have to do with World War Two?" Jennifer asked.

"They played an important role," Wagner said. "They provided troops for the defense of the Panama Canal, and they nationalized all the airlines, which until that time had been under German control. In addition, they declared war on Germany in 1943."

"Interesting," Jennifer said. "Go on, Don, I'm sorry about the interruption."

"No problem," Don said. "But, as you can see, the Cortina name has been prominent in Colombia's history for many years. In addition to being a general, Ricardo is a former judge. He is a wealthy and powerful man who could just live out the rest of his days in comfort, but he has chosen to serve his country in the way he feels is best for it."

"You said there were two?" Chris asked.

"Yes, the nephew is Esteban Cortina. Esteban is a journalist for the Cali newspaper. He and his uncle Ricardo head up an organization known as the LBC, *Libere Brigada de Colombia*, or the Free Colombia Brigade."

"What have you been able to find out about the LBC?"

"Not a whole lot. Evidently, they didn't even organize until after Mendoza announced his intention to secede from Colombia. They are still in the formative stage."

"Don, what about Katy Correal? Were you able to find out anything about her?" John asked.

"Her parents were killed by the FARC when she was fourteen. She went into a government-sponsored home until she was an adult. She was Miss Colombia in the Miss World contest ten years ago, and earned her living as a model for a while after that."

"Miss Colombia?"

"She is a very beautiful woman," Don said. "I found this picture of her on the Internet, and printed it." He handed John a picture.

John gave a low whistle. "I'll say this for Brian. He had taste."

"After her modeling stint, she went to school, got a degree in administration, and now works for the Ministry of Agriculture."

"Any known associations that might trigger some interest?" John asked.

"None. She's as clean as a whistle."

"Why are you interested in her?" Mike asked.

"Why is he interested, are you kidding? Look at her, she's beautiful. I think he's just trying to set up a date," Jennifer teased.

Chris looked at the picture as well. "Yeah, well, good luck. Any time I've ever asked someone out who looks like that, she couldn't go because she had to wash her hair or something."

The others laughed.

"I don't know," John said. "She was close to Brian. You never can tell, we might be able to use her in one way or another."

"I've been answering all the questions," Don said. "Now I have one."

"Shoot," John invited.

"How are we going? Are we going to charter a plane?"

John looked over at Wagner. "You want to take this, Wagner?"

"You'll fly down commercially," Wagner said. "You'll go in teams of two, though you will maintain separation during the flight."

"When do we leave?" Linda asked.

"Jennifer and I will leave DFW tomorrow morning at eleven thirty-five," John said, taking over then. "Wagner has the schedule worked out for the rest of you."

Chapter 4

DFW

John and Jennifer boarded separately at Dallas, and sat at opposite ends of the plane. It was a little under an hour to Houston. After a layover of one and a half hours in Houston, they boarded a 757 for Bogota, again in separate seats, for the seven-hour flight.

Bogota Airport, Bogata, Colombia

"Business or pleasure, senor?" the customs official asked at the Bogota Airport. He had John's open luggage in front of him, and a woman was going through it.

"Business," John replied. "I'm a novelist and I am down here on research for my new book."

"A novelist? Well, I am honored, senor. Do you have any drugs or weapons with you?"

"No."

"Do you have any plant life that would be detrimental to the indigenous plant life of Colombia?"

"No."

"And how long will you be with us?"

"I'm not sure," John said. "As long as the research takes."

The woman who was searching through John's bag closed it, then nodded at the ~~customs~~ official, who gave John a pamphlet.

"As you know, senor, Colombia has many dangers for the unwary visitor. This is mostly due to illegal drugs. Our government is very strict about the illegal possession of drugs, and if you are caught dealing in drugs, the penalty will be very harsh."

"As it should be," John said.

"Then we can depend upon you to follow our laws?"

"Yes."

"This printed material will tell you what places you should avoid."

"Thank you."

"You are cleared, senor. I hope you enjoy your visit to beautiful Colombia."

With his luggage in hand, John left customs, then reported to the check-in counter for the next leg of his flight. He was informed there would be a two-hour-and-fifteen-minute wait before departure.

After checking his luggage through, John started toward the bar. So far, he and Jennifer had purposely maintained a separation between them. Jennifer had actually gotten through customs ahead of John and had already checked her baggage through. Out of the corner of his eye, John saw that she had found a seat in the gate area and was sitting there patiently, reading a book.

John had been in the airport bar for about ten minutes when a man came up to stand right beside him. This immediately aroused John's attention because there was plenty of room at the bar. He went on alert.

The man ordered a beer.

"Dumb bartender," the man said under his breath. "The service in Mexico City is much better."

For a moment, John hesitated, then he realized

that this wasn't just casual conversation, that it was a password challenge. If he didn't answer the challenge properly, he could be killed.

"But it's worse in Phoenix," John replied.

"I am Carlos," the man said. "They have taken your woman."

"What?" John asked. He was not certain that he heard Carlos correctly.

"The woman you are traveling with has been kidnapped," Carlos repeated. "You'll find her at this address."

John felt Carlos put something rather heavy in his jacket pocket. After that the man got his beer and walked away. Not until he was sitting at a table on the other side of the bar did John reach down into his pocket.

He felt a pistol and a matchbook cover. Pulling out the matchbook cover, he opened it and read the note inside.

> Four Points
> Avenida Eldorado 69c
> Room 406

He glanced back toward the table but Carlos was gone. Quickly, John left the bar and stepped out into the main waiting room area. He looked into the gate area where he had last seen Jennifer, but she wasn't there!

"Shit!" John said. He looked at the matchbook cover again. Four Points. Four Points. What the hell was Four Points?

Then, seeing the room number, he realized that it had to be a hotel.

Out in front of the airport, John saw a taxi just pulling up at a passenger pickup zone. Two young men were about to get into the cab. Without saying a word to them, John grabbed them both by their collars and pulled them away.

"Hey!" *Qué hace usted?*" one of the two men shouted angrily.

"*Tome el siguiente taxi,*" John said as he slid into the backseat and closed the door. He showed the address to the driver. "*Quiero ir aquí,*" he said.

"Senor, you asked the others to take another taxi, but they were before you," the driver protested.

"You speak English."

"*Sí.*"

"Good," John said. He took the pistol from his pocket and pointed it at the driver. "Then you will understand me when I ask you again. Take me to the address on the matchbook cover."

"*Sí, sí!*" the driver replied, and he pulled away from the curb, even as the two young men had started toward it again. John turned to look through the back window and saw that both of them were showing him their middle finger.

John laughed quietly at their frustration. He didn't blame them, he would be pissed too. But he had no choice, he couldn't afford the time to wait in line for another taxi.

Turning back around, John contemplated the last few minutes. Obviously their mission was already compromised, or the people who took her wouldn't have been lying in wait for her. But that wasn't the whole of it. They also knew about him; otherwise Carlos would not have been able to contact him at the bar.

How did they know about the mission? And for that matter, how did they know who was who?

Fortunately, the hotel proved to be only about five minutes from the airport. The cab stopped in front of the hotel, and the driver turned toward John.

From the fear in his eyes, it was obvious that he still considered John to be a danger to him.

"Here," John said, giving the driver a one-hundred-dollar bill for a tab that calculated to no more than eight dollars.

The driver looked at the bill in confusion. "Senor, I don't have enough money to make change for this," he said.

"Keep the change," John said as he hopped from the cab.

"*Sí!* Okay!" the driver shouted happily as John bounded up the driveway to the old, restored hotel.

John didn't even go to the front desk. Instead, he went straight to the elevator, stepped into it, and pushed the door-close button even as someone was hurrying to catch the elevator.

"*Pare el elevador!*" the hurrying guest shouted in Spanish, but John continued to hold the button and the guest didn't make it.

John took the elevator to the fourth floor. As soon as the doors opened, he pulled the panel, then jerked some wires. The elevator descended automatically to the basement where it would remain until repaired.

As soon as the doors shut, John turned around to see a bellhop pushing a baggage cart. The bellhop was staring at him with eyes open wide in shock.

"*Senor, qué hizo usted?*" the bellhop asked, surprised at seeing him send the elevator down in such a way.

John pulled his pistol and pointed it at the bellhop, who jumped back in fear and put his hands up. John motioned him into a housecleaning closet, then closed the door behind them. There, John tied and gagged him.

"Sorry 'bout this," he said. "But I don't want anyone reporting that elevator just ye

That taken care of, John took the bellhop's master

key, then stepped back into the hall. When he reached room 408 he opened the door.

An old lady was inside, watching television, and she looked up in surprise when John walked in.

"*Soy con el mantenimiento de hotel,*" John said, indicating that he was here on official maintenance business for the hotel.

The old woman smiled, nodded, and went back to watching TV. When John raised the window and stepped out onto the ledge, she didn't give him a second thought.

John climbed out onto the ledge, then eased up to the window of room 406. Looking inside, he saw Jennifer's reflection in the mirror. She was lying on the bed, her hands and feet bound with duct tape.

There were three men in the room and John gasped when he recognized one of them. It was Carlos, the same man who had told him that Jennifer was captured!

Damn! he thought. This was a setup!

John punched out the magazine of the pistol Carlos had given him. He wasn't surprised that it was empty. When he checked the chamber, he saw that it was empty as well.

All right, he would just have to work around that.

The three men were staring at the door, guns at the ready, waiting for John to come bursting into the room. As John continued to scan the room, he saw, by the reflection in the mirror, that Jennifer had seen him. Their eyes met.

Because of ongoing classes, every member of the Code Name Team was fluent in Spanish, French, German, Italian, and Portuguese. In addition, they all knew universal sign language, and John took advantage of that fact now to sign to Jennifer.

"Get one of the men to come to the window," he said by sign.

Jennifer nodded.

"Would someone please adjust the air-conditioning?" Jennifer called. "It's hot in here."

When nobody responded, she asked again. "Please, I'm burning up. If you're going to kill me, at least let me be comfortable until you do."

Carlos laughed. "She wants to be comfortable until we kill her. She is a funny woman. Pedro, make it cooler."

"*Es frío en aquí,*" Pedro replied, wrapping his arms around himself and shivering.

"I don't care how cold it is, just do it," Carlos ordered, more firmly this time.

Grumbling, Pedro walked back to the air-conditioner controls, which were just under the window. John waited until Pedro was bent over the unit, then, using the gun as a hammer, smashed through the glass.

Pedro rose up in shock, just as John leaped in through the window. Using the advantage of surprise, John grabbed Pedro, and Pedro's gun, then spun Pedro around, holding the Colombian between him and the other two men.

Carlos and the other man fired, and John could feel Pedro's body jerking as he was hit by their bullets. John returned fire, killing both of them. When the shooting ended, all three Colombians lay dead on the hotel room floor.

"There are at least two more," Jennifer said as John began cutting the tape from her wrists and ankles.

"Where are they, do you know?"

"They're out in the hallway somewhere. I'm sure they heard the shots and they'll be here any second."

John jerked the bedspread from the bed, then

pulled off the blanket and gave it to her. "Here," he said. "You'll need this."

"For what?" she asked, looking at the blanket in confusion.

"You'll see."

John jerked off the sheet and moved to the door. Opening it, he saw two men at the far end of the hall coming toward the room.

"Come on, let's go!" John shouted. He stepped out into the hall and fired at the two men. They jumped back into one of the alcoves, out of his line of fire.

"Head for the elevator on the right!" John shouted.

"Damn! I hope you don't plan to wait for the elevator?"

"Not exactly," John said as they reached it. Grabbing the doors, he forced them open, exposing nothing but the elevator cables.

"Oh, shit," Jennifer said. "Please tell me you don't mean what I think you mean."

The men began firing at John and Jennifer from the alcove down the hall, and the bullets started slamming into the elevator doors.

"Go!" John shouted.

"Ohhhhhh, shiiiiit!" Jennifer shouted as, using the blanket to protect her hands, she leaped onto the cables and started sliding down. John jumped on right behind her and as he did so, the elevator doors slammed shut. Even as they were sliding down, they could hear bullets punching through the elevator doors overhead.

John and Jennifer slid all the way down to the basement.

"Are you all right?" John asked when they hit the top of the elevator.

"Yeah, I'm fine," Jennifer said. "But if it's all the same to you, next time let's just take the stairs."

John opened the hatch on top of the elevator and then he and Jennifer dropped down inside. There, John pried the doors open. "Let's get out of here," he said.

For the flight from Bogota to Cali, John got his seat changed so that he and Jennifer sat together.

"No need in trying to pretend we don't know each other now," John explained. "We've already been made."

"How did they find out so fast?" Jennifer asked.

John shook his head. "I don't have the slightest idea. But the first thing we are going to have to do is change the password challenges."

"We can't do that," Jennifer said. "We've already put the word out to our contacts down here."

"That's it," John said.

"What?"

"That's how we were compromised. One of our contacts down here is a mole."

The flight from Bogota to Cali was a short one and John was on the satellite phone as soon as they landed.

"Wagner," he said, "we've been compromised."

There was a moment of silence. "Do we need to abort?" Wagner asked.

"No, but tell the others to be on their toes. Especially with the password and challenge."

"Will do."

John punched the phone off, then looked over at Jennifer. "I know he is wondering what happened, but the less we say over the phone, the better off we'll be, I think."

"I agree," Jennifer said.

Collecting their luggage, they hailed a taxi in front of the airport.

Cali, Colombia

Manuel Gaviria watched the man and woman get into the taxi, then he took out his cell phone and called a number.

"Two of them are here," he said. "They just took a taxi from the front of the airport."

"Good," the voice on the other end of the cell phone said. "Let me know when the others arrive."

Buenaventura, Colombia, Mendoza's estate

Luiz Mendoza hung up the telephone, then picked up his drink.

"Gato, you are sure I can depend upon Carlos?" Mendoza asked.

"Yes, I am positive. Carlos is a good man," Rodriguez "Gato" Valdez replied.

Mendoza pointed to the telephone. "That was Raol," he said. "He reports that Barrone and a woman have just arrived at the Dugger's and Green Hotel."

"What?" Gato replied. "But how can that be? They were to have been stopped in Bogota."

"They are there because Carlos failed his mission," Mendoza said.

"No," Gato said. "That can't be."

"You have let me down, Gato," Mendoza said. "How can I depend upon you, if you let me down?"

"I promise, Luiz, it will not happen again," Gato said.

Mendoza held up his finger. "When we were children together, you could call me Luiz. But now I think you should address me as El Presidente."

"But we are not yet a country, so you are not yet—" Gato halted his reply in mid statement when he saw the glare of disapproval in Mendoza's eyes. "Of course, El Presidente," he said, with a slight bow of his head.

"If you wish to occupy a position of authority in my government, then you are going to have to provide me with more dependable people than Carlos."

"I am sorry, El Presidente. There will be no more mistakes, and I shall see to it that Carlos pays dearly," Gato said.

"There is no need for that," Mendoza said. He picked up his glass and took a drink.

"You are being very generous to Carlos," Gato said. "It is a true act of your mercy."

"Carlos has already paid," Mendoza said. "He is dead. He failed, and Barrone and the woman are in Cali."

"But, Excellente, you said yourself that the U.S. Government will not do anything."

"That is true. The U.S. Government is doing nothing, but they are allowing some of their citizens to do it, privately."

"Mercenaries?"

"Yes, you might call them that."

Gato laughed. "The U.S. Government is sending in mercenaries? How dangerous can that be?"

"I don't know," Mendoza replied, staring back over the rim of his glass. "Suppose you ask Carlos that?"

Chapter 5

Cali, Colombia

John and Jennifer took rooms at the hotel Dugger's and Green, then waited for the others to join them. While they were waiting, John visited the Ministry of Agriculture's offices in Cali.

A uniformed man behind a desk in the lobby looked up as John approached.

"*Necesita usted la ayuda?*"

"Yes, you can help me," John replied. "Do you speak English?"

"Yes," the guard answered.

"I am looking for Senorita Katy Correal. I believe she is employed here."

The guard tapped a few computer keys, then got the name. He picked up the phone and called.

"*Hay un hombre para ver usted, senorita Correal,*" he said into the phone. Then he covered the mouthpiece and looked up at John. "Your name and purpose of visit, please?"

"My name is John Barrone. I was a very good friend of Brian Skipper."

The guard repeated the message, then said, "*Sí,*" and hung up the phone.

"She will be here in a moment."

"Thank you."

There was a sofa against one wall of the lobby, and John sat down while he waited. Through the glass front of the building, he could see the traffic on Avenida 3, and across the road, the Cali River. There were several outdoor vendors on the bank of the river, some selling fresh fruit, others vegetables, and still others, freshly caught fish. Traffic was heavy, though most of the vehicles were commercial vehicles in the form of trucks, buses, and taxis.

He heard the bell ring at the elevator and when the doors opened, a woman stepped out. He recognized her at once as Katy Correal, though none of her photographs did her justice. She was an exceptionally beautiful woman with long black hair, dark, almost almond-shaped eyes, and smooth, olive skin.

"You are Brian's friend?" she asked as she started toward John, who had stood to greet her.

"Yes," John replied.

"I am very pleased to meet you," Katy said, extending her hand. John shook it.

"Thank you," John said.

"I have taken the afternoon off," Katy said. "Would you like to go somewhere for coffee, or a drink?"

John smiled. "In Colombia, one must have coffee," he said.

"I know just the place."

John held the door open for her as they left. "Should I get us a taxi?" he asked.

Katy shook her head. "There is no need. The café is very near."

As they walked, the smells of the river drifted over to them. It was only a faintly fishy smell, not nearly as strong as the smells he had experienced in other parts of the world. In fact, it even added a bit to the exotic atmosphere. And when they passed several stands selling cut flowers, their sweet aroma replaced that of the fish.

"In here," she said, pointing toward a building.

The café was called Dukes, and it was on the second floor. It was more than just a café, it was a jazz/blues bar and a piano and bass were playing softly on a little stage at the back of the café.

"Señorita Correal, *Bienvenidos a Duques*," the maitre d' said when they went inside.

"Hello, Jorges," Katy replied in English. Could we have a table near the window?"

"Yes, of course," Jorges said, switching to English as well.

Jorges led them through the little café to a small table for two that was right against the window. Because it was elevated, they could not only see the river, they could actually look down onto it and see the boats, both working boats and pleasure boats.

"If you don't think it will ruin your dinner, you might try a piece of coffee loaf cake," Katy suggested. "It is delicious."

"Sure, I'll try it. It sounds good," John said.

Katy ordered for both of them, and a moment later the waiter returned with their coffee and cake.

"So," Katy said, "you say you were Brian's friend. Where did you know him?"

"We were in school together," John said.

"You were close?"

"He was the best man at my wedding."

"Ahh, so you are married?"

"No," John said. "My wife is dead."

Katy reached across the table and put her hand on John's. "I'm sorry to hear that."

"It has been a long time."

"But you still miss her."

"Yes, very much."

"I know how it is. I still miss Brian. But tell me, Senor Barrone—"

"John," John corrected.

"John," she said, though the J was soft and his name came out as Shon. "How did you know about me? I didn't think Brian told anyone about us."

"Oh, he talked about you all right, and I must say, he wasn't exaggerating when he spoke of your beauty."

Katy smiled and reached up to brush a fall of hair back from her face.

"Now you are embarrassing me," she said.

"I don't mean to embarrass you. And surely you are aware that you are a very beautiful woman."

"Yes, well, I try to get beyond that," she said. "I'm curious, John. Did you come all the way to Colombia just to talk about Brian?"

"Sort of," John said. "I'm trying to find out more about how he died."

"He was murdered by the FARC," Katy said.

"Yes, I know that is the police report. But his family hired me to find out more if I could."

"You were hired by his family? Why would they hire you?"

"Well, I'm a private detective," John said. "And sometimes I can find out more information than the police, simply by digging deeper into the subject. For example, did the police interview you about Brian?"

"No," Katy admitted.

"Well then, you see, I'm already ahead of the game."

"But I don't know anything more than what I heard," Katy insisted. "He was murdered by the FARC."

"What about the Independent Pangean Group?" John asked.

"What about them?"

"It's my understanding that there is a broad-based movement to have part of Colombia secede in order to establish the new country of Pangea. Are you aware of that?"

"Yes, of course. Everyone in Colombia knows about the Pangean movement. But what does that have to do with Brian's being killed?"

"Perhaps they felt he was a danger to the movement," John suggested.

"How could he be a danger? He was an agriculture consultant."

"I'll ask you the same question. Why would the FARC attack him?"

"Because part of his job was to find and eliminate coca, poppy, and marijuana fields. That represented a danger to the FARC."

"Wouldn't it also represent a danger to the Pangean independence movement, since it threatens their main source of income?"

"I suppose," Katy admitted.

"What do you know about the *Libere Brigada de Colombia?*"

Katy's eyes narrowed, and she grew defensive. "You ask a lot of questions, John," she said.

"That's my job," John replied. "So, you do know about the Free Colombia Brigade?"

"Yes, I know about them."

"Is it possible that they had something to do with killing Brian?"

"Anything is possible," Katy said.

"So, you believe it *was* the LBC?"

"I didn't say that. I said anything was possible."

"Umm, you were right," John said, finishing his cake. "This really was delicious."

"Thank you," Katy said.

"Thank you for suggesting it."

"No," Katy said. "I mean thank you for changing the subject. I find that Brian's death is still too painful for me to talk about."

"I understand," John said.

It took nearly a week for the entire team to reach Cali, and the others spread out all over town, staying not only at Dugger's and Green, but also the Casa Del Alferez, the Pacifco Royal, and the Torre De Cali.

When Mike Rojas and Linda Marsh arrived, the last two to do so, the team gathered in John's room.

"Okay, boss," Chris said. "We're all here now. What's our next move?"

"Chris, I want you and Linda to go see Marin. According to our source, he is the one who can supply us with weapons—"

Chris interrupted. "What kind of weapons?"

"I doubt that he can get us an eight-inch howitzer, or an Apache. But I suspect he can get just about anything else we will need."

"What about vehicles?"

"He can supply those too."

"That's going to take a lot of money."

John nodded, then picked up a small canvas bag. He took out some socks, underwear, a shaving kit, and a few T-shirts, then removed the bottom of the bag, disclosing a false bottom. That done, he turned the bag upside down, dumping the remaining contents on the bed. Several bound stacks of money tumbled out. Each stack contained a hundred one-hundred-dollar bills.

"Holy shit!" Chris said.

"How much money is that?" Linda asked.

"Half a million dollars," John said. "Make it go as far as you can."

Chris picked up a few of the bundles, then let them fall back down. "Half a million?"

"Give or take ten thousand," John said.

"Ha, give or take ten thousand my ass," Chris said. "Knowing Wagner, he made you sign for this in blood." He chuckled. "I think we can work with this."

"I thought you might be able to. Don, you set up your computers and satellite phones. We aren't getting any official help from Uncle, but my contact gave me a few codes and passwords that might be of some help." He gave Don Yee a little notebook and Don looked through it.

"Wow," Don said. "Some help? I would say so. This will allow me to tap into all the government satellite feeds: images, telephone conversations, radio transmissions . . . this is a bonanza."

"Yeah, I thought you might like that," John said.

"What about Mike and me?" Paul asked.

"I want you two to wander through town, hit a few bars, listen in to a few conversations. I want to know how much support this secession actually has."

"Whoa, wait a minute," Chris said. "Linda and I go round up weapons, Paul and Mike hit the local bars?"

"Yeah," Paul said. "It hardly seems fair, does it? But if it has to be done, I guess Mike and I can force ourselves into doing it."

The others laughed.

"What about you, Chief? Where are you going to be?" Mike asked.

"Jennifer and I are going to church."

Chris laughed. "Church?"

"Yeah," John said without further explanation.

Chapter 6

Paul and Mike were sitting at a table in the back of the room nursing a beer and observing the others in the bar. There was a flag behind the bar top. The top half of the flag was yellow, the bottom half was divided into two horizontal bars. The top bar was blue, the red.

"Get that flag down," someone demanded angrily.

"Why should I take down the flag of my country?" the bartender replied.

"Because that is no longer the flag of your country. This is the flag of your country."

The agitator held up a new flag. It was orange, with a white circle in the middle of a black St. Andrews cross. Inside the circle was a four-pointed black star.

"This is the flag of Pangea."

"We are not Pangea yet," the bartender said.

The man with the flag took out a pistol and pointed it at the bartender.

"I say we are Pangea now," he said. "Take that flag down and put this one up."

"*Sí*," the bartender said, complying with the order.

"Everyone stand!" the man with the gun ordered.

Nobody complied, and the man pointed his gun straight up and pulled the trigger. The sound of the gunshot filled the bar.

"I said stand!" he shouted angrily.

Everyone stood and faced the new flag.

"Salute!" the man with the gun ordered.

With varying degrees of enthusiasm, the bar patrons saluted.

Satisfied that the new flag was getting the proper respect, the gunman left. After he left, the bartender called out to one of the customers near the front door, "Is he gone?"

"*Sí.*"

The bartender spat on the new flag and the others in the bar cheered.

Paul looked at Mike.

"I wouldn't say this new country of theirs is enjoying that much support, would you?"

"That would be my take," Mike said.

Chris and Linda got out of the taxi in front of a bicycle shop. The front of the shop was open, and just inside were several score bicycles, some new, many used. In addition, a worktable stretched along each of the three walls. Spread out on the table were hundreds of bicycle parts. At least three bicycle mechanics were working at the tables.

A tall, thin man with a bushy mustache and wire-rim glasses greeted them.

"Yes, may I help you?"

"I don't wish to buy, but I would like to rent a bicycle for two if you have a green one. However, a red one will do."

The smile left the bicycle man's face.

"I am sorry, senor. We have only blue and yellow."

That was the correct response.

"You are Viktor Marin?" Chris asked.

"I am," the bicycle man replied.

"Senor Marin, I was told that I could do business with you, if the price was right."

"*Sí*," Marin said. "You can buy anything in my shop if you pay for it."

"I'm looking for a very special vehicle," Chris said. "One that does not need roads. Perhaps a HumVee?"

"HumVees cost a great deal of money, senor. Especially down here."

"Yes, well, I have a great deal of money," Chris said.

When Chris mentioned money, Marin's face became animated for the first time.

"How much money?" he asked.

"I have as much money as I will need," Chris replied. "But I want two of them, and they must be armor-equipped, also fitted with two-way radios and GPS."

"I see." Marin stroked his jaw for a moment. "I can help you, senor, but not in this place. You must come with me."

Chris and Linda followed Marin through a door at the back of the shop. Behind the shop was a vehicle under a tarpaulin cover. Marin jerked the cover off to reveal a mint-condition, vintage Rolls Royce.

"Hmm, the bicycle business must be good," Chris said.

Suddenly Marin spun around and, when he did so, there was a pistol in his hand. He was smiling broadly, until he noticed that both Chris and Linda were holding pistols pointed at him. The smile left his face, to be replaced by one of shock and fear.

Chris held his left hand out, palm up. "Give me the gun," he said. "Butt first."

Marin laughed weakly.

"Senor, I would not want you to get the wrong impression," he said. "I was just being careful."

"Yes. So are we," Chris said.

"Do you still want the HumVees?" Marin asked, his face now twisted and frightened.

"Yes. Provided we can come to a deal."

"You mean . . . you will not try to steal them from me?"

"Why the hell should we do that?" Chris asked. "From time to time there may be other things that we need. Who better to supply the things we need than you?"

"*Sí*, senor! *Sí!*" Marin said, now with a very broad smile. "Come, I will take you."

"Wait, she will get into the car first," Chris said, nodding toward Linda. Linda got into the back right behind the driver's seat.

"Now you," John said.

Marin got in.

Not until Linda was holding her pistol just inches away from the back of Marin's head did Chris get into the car.

"Now drive us to the place where we can buy the HumVees . . . and, perhaps, a few other products as well," Chris ordered.

"*Sí*," Marin replied as he started the car. "I think we will do much business together. It is always good to do business with a cautious man."

They drove out of the city and into encroaching jungles. They had been driving for nearly half an hour when they approached a roadblock.

"Senor, you said you have a lot of money?" Marin asked.

"Yes."

"Then you must be prepared to use some of it now," he said.

"What is this?" Linda asked.

"This is a roadblock manned by soldiers of the revolution."

"The Pangean revolution?"

"Yes."

"A roadblock? What are they looking for?"

Both Chris and Marin laughed.

"Money!" they said as one.

"Extortion at roadblocks is one of the ways they pay for their operation," Chris said. "Robbery, kidnapping, and blackmail are some of the other ways."

"And drug trafficking?" Linda asked.

"*Sí.* They sell the drugs to overseas markets."

"What about weapons?" Chris asked.

"Oh, no, senor, you don't want to go to them for weapons. I can supply you with whatever you need."

Chris and Linda looked at each other and smiled.

Marin stopped at the roadblock and put his window down. A man wearing khaki trousers and shirt and a red bandana leaned down to talk to them.

"*Dónde va usted?*" he asked.

"*Estos son norteamericanos. Ellos son recién visitan Colombia,*" Marin said.

"*Norteamericanos,* eh? If they are just married, why is the man riding in front with you?" the man asked in English.

"*Mi marido se enferma cuando él viaja en un coche,*" Linda said, speaking perfect and Colombian-accented Spanish.

The man in the red scarf chuckled, then looked at Chris.

"Your wife says you get carsick. Is this true?"

"*Sí,*" Chris said, and he put his hand to his mouth as if barely able to control his nausea.

"I thought you were *norteamericano,*" Red Bandana said to Linda.

"I am. But my parents are Colombian and I have been here many times to visit my grandparents and this beautiful country."

"You go to visit them now?"

"No," Linda said. "They were killed by government soldiers."

Red Bandana nodded. "*Sí*. The government soldiers are evil."

"My husband and I would like to donate to your cause," she said. "How much do you think would be a good amount to show our sympathy is with you?"

"One hundred dollars?" Red Banana replied.

"Darling, give the man one hundred dollars," Linda said.

"But, sweetheart, we have very little money left. We will not be able to do as many things as we hoped while we are here," Chris said.

"So, we will eat less. These men are genuine heroes of Colombia."

Chris made a pained show of giving money to Red Bandana. The rebel took the money, then stepped back from the car.

"Let these people through unharmed!" he shouted down the road, then waved them on.

They were half a mile beyond the roadblock before Marin spoke.

"You told the rebel you had very little money."

"Yes."

"But you told me you had enough money to buy the HumVees."

"If I had told the rebel that I had a lot of money with me, he would have taken it," Chris said. "Then there would be none left for you."

"*Sí*," Marin said. "*Sí*. You did a wise thing."

Chris turned in the seat and smiled at Linda. "What about you, sweetheart?" he asked, jokingly. "Did your 'darling' do a wise thing?"

Linda laughed. "Enjoy the banter, Chris. It's as close as you will ever get."

They turned off the paved road, then drove for some distance up a dirt road that continued to get narrower and more twisting until finally they came to a compound in the middle of the forest. The compound was surrounded by a high chain-link fence, topped with barbed wire. There was a guard at the gate and he started toward the car, but seeing Marin, he went back to the guardhouse and opened the gate.

Inside the perimeter was a park of military-type vehicles, from the latest HumVees to three-quarter and half-ton trucks of the type Chris could remember from his own days in the military. In fact, though they had been painted over, he could still see the shadowy markings on the bumpers that let him know that they were surplus U.S. military.

The bumper of the three-quarter nearest him read: USA 7 DIV 32 RGT 1 BN A-12.

That was the Seventh Infantry Division, Thirty-second Regiment, First Battalion, A Company. Chris had once been a part of the Seventh Division. That was several years ago, and he wondered, in passing, if he had ever seen this specific truck driving around at Camp Casey, just outside Tong Du Chon, Korea.

The HumVees were not surplus. That was good. Chris was willing to pay well, but he wanted something for his money.

"As you can see," Marin said with a sweep of his arm, "we have quite a variety to choose from."

"Who do you sell to?" Linda asked.

"To anyone who has the money," Marin replied.

"To the revolutionaries?"

"*Sí,* they are our biggest customers."

"To the local authorities?"

"*Sí.*"

"To the drug cartel?"

"Yes."

"So you will sell to anyone?"

"I am in business, senorita," Marin said. "I cannot afford to take sides, for to do so would cut my market. Surely you can understand that."

"You said something earlier about being able to supply us with weapons," Chris said. "What do you have?"

Marin smiled and made a motion with his hand. "Come with me," he said.

Chris and Linda followed him through the compound to a large building. Inside was one huge room, filled with tables and racks of weapons.

Chris whistled. "You've got quite an arsenal here," he said.

"Thanks, I'm rather proud of it," Marin said. He held out his arm. "As I said, we have many weapons. Choose what you want."

John and Jennifer sat halfway back on the left side of the sanctuary as Archbishop Duarte consecrated the elements on the altar table. When the elements were consecrated and offered to the people, Jennifer, who was Catholic, joined the line of worshipers to approach the altar. John, who was not Catholic, remained in his seat.

"The body of Christ," the priest said as he placed the wafer on Jennifer's tongue.

After the service was concluded, John and Jennifer waited until everyone was gone. Then, when the archbishop went into the confessional booth, Jennifer got up, genuflected, and went in as well. The window was opened.

Instead of "Bless me, Father, for I have sinned," Jennifer said, "The nation is in peril."

"It is a time for patriots," the priest responded.

Jennifer eased the hammer down on her pistol and slipped it back into her purse, thankful that the archbishop had given the correct response.

"You have information for me?" Jennifer asked through the grate, speaking quietly.

"Esteban Cortina," the archbishop replied. "He is a reporter, and you will find him at the *El Pais* newspaper. Tell him these words, exactly as I am saying them to you."

Jennifer got out a pencil and paper and took notes.

"Senor Cortina, I am a reporter for the *Mobile Register*. I wish to do a story about the music of Colombia. I hear that you can tell me many delightful tales."

Duarte paused for a moment, then said, "Do you have that, exactly as I spoke the words?"

Jennifer read back to him, "Senor Cortina, I am a reporter for the *Mobile Register*. I wish to do a story about the music of Colombia. I hear that you can tell me many delightful tales."

"Yes, that is good. He will respond, 'I once visited Mobile. It is a beautiful place.'"

"I know of Esteban Cortina," Jennifer said, thinking of the briefing they had received before leaving Texas.

"Yes. Esteban is the nephew of Ricardo Cortina, a true patriot. Ricardo Cortina wishes to take our beautiful country back from the criminals. He is a courageous man who will welcome your help in his fight."

It did not escape Jennifer's notice that the archbishop said that Cortina wanted their help, rather than offering to help them. That was good. That meant that, although Cortina would welcome the Code Name Team as a participant, he did not regard them as the principal. He was willing to take on the lion's share of the struggle, and would do it all by himself if that became necessary.

"May God go with you and those who are with you in this battle to save our country," Duarte said.

"Thank you, Father."

As Jennifer left the confessional booth, she passed in front of the altar where, once again, she genuflected. She started back up the aisle, nodding at John, who joined her at the narthex.

"Did you get what we need from him?"

"Yes," Jennifer said.

Five minutes later, Jennifer and John were standing on the corner in front of the church, waiting for a taxi. They watched as a large black limousine came to a stop in front of the church. A driver got out, walked around to open the back door, and waited as Archbishop Durate came down the steps.

"He is a good man," Jennifer said quietly.

"Yes, he is," John agreed. "It's just too bad that there aren't several like him in Colombia's congress."

Jennifer chuckled. "Why limit it to the Congress of Colombia?" she said. "We could use a few men like him in our own Congress."

"You've got that right."

Suddenly two motorcycles turned off the road and got onto the sidewalk.

"John!" Jennifer said.

"I see them."

They both watched the motorcycles roar toward the prelate, but, as neither of them was armed, there was nothing they could do.

The staccato bark of automatic gunfire could be heard above the roar of motorcycle engines.

Even from their position on the corner half a

block away, they could see the spray of red as the archbishop went down. The driver, in terror, ran around to the far side of the car and crouched down behind it as the two gunmen continued to spray bullets into Durate's now-still body.

Satisfied that their job was accomplished, the two motorcyclists tossed their guns aside, then rode away amidst the roar of engines and the squeal of tires. The front wheels of both machines were lifted into the air as they sped away.

For just a moment everyone on the street and around the church stood in shocked silence, staring in disbelief at what they had just seen. An archbishop had been killed before their very eyes.

John and Jennifer ran toward the fallen priest and were the first there. John knelt beside him, but even before he took the man's pulse, he knew he was dead. He looked up at Jennifer and shook his head sadly.

They heard the sound of the motorcycles again.

"They are coming back!" someone shouted.

John ran toward one of the guns the cyclists had discarded after the shooting, and Jennifer, seeing what he was doing, ran after the other one.

The two bikers, for intimidation as much as anything else, came back toward the scene of their shooting at full speed. Both were bent low over the handlebars as their bikes topped seventy miles an hour.

At the last minute John and Jennifer stepped out into the street and aimed at the bikers. The bikers saw that they were being targeted and they made a desperate attempt to avoid it. In their desperation, one of them collided with the other.

Neither John nor Jennifer was required to fire a shot. Both bikes went down, then slid, their machines sending out a veritable shower of sparks. The riders were trapped with their bikes and John and Jennifer watched in horror as they skidded toward the archbishop's limo.

The crowd that had gathered around the slain prelate scattered and ran, just as the two bikes slammed into the car. There was a hesitation of no more than a couple of seconds, then the car exploded in a huge ball of flame.

The two bikers could be seen burning and one of them raised his arm in agony, then dropped it back down. Both of them were taken out without a shot being fired.

When the team gathered one more time in John's suite at the Dugger's and Green Hotel, they gave their reports on their activities for the day. John and Jennifer spoke first, sharing the information with the others that Father Duarte had been killed, and that they had actually witnessed it.

"I would hate to think that we were the cause of his death," Linda said.

"How would we be the cause?" Paul asked.

"Well, by setting up the meeting with him," Linda answered.

"Oh yeah, I see what you mean."

John shook his head. "We weren't the cause. The men who shot him were the cause. And Father Duarte was actively opposing Pangea, so they would have gotten to him eventually, whether we set up a meeting with him or not."

"Yeah, I guess that's right," Linda agreed. "And at least you and Jennifer managed to take out the assholes who shot him."

"Well, they took themselves out, actually. Now, what about the rest of you?" John asked.

Paul told of his and Mike's tour of the bars.

"Were you able to get a gauge of the people?" John asked. "Do you have an idea of what they think of the secession?"

"Yeah," Paul said. "They are against it."

Mike told the vignette of the bartender spitting on the new flag, and the other patrons in the bar cheering his action.

"That sounds encouraging," John said. He had saved Chris's report for last. "Now, Chris, what about you, did you have any luck?"

Chris looked at Linda, and they both smiled broadly. Then Chris took a folded piece of paper from his pocket and began reading. "HumVee vehicles, two each. M-60 machine guns, two each. M-59 grenade launchers, four each. M-16 rifles, twenty-four each. M-24 SWS rifle, one each. Glock 33 .357 magnum pistols, eight each. Two-way satellite radios, ten each. Tracer ammunition, caliber 7.62, one thousand rounds. Ball ammunition, caliber 7.62, five thousand rounds. MREs, one thousand."

"Five hundred MREs?" Jennifer asked. "You actually think we are going to need five hundred meals ready to eat?"

"Well, we got two hundred fifty for us, and two hundred fifty for Don," Linda explained.

"That should just about hold me," Don said, and the others laughed, for Don's appetite was legend among them.

"What's next?" Mike asked.

"Tomorrow, we visit our contact at the newspaper office, then we move into the field," John said. "Our revolution is about to begin."

Chapter 7

The newspaper offices could have been in Dallas, St. Louis, Baltimore, or Hong Kong. It was the premiere news organ of a large, metropolitan area and as such, had the same feel and excitement all newspapers have.

A counter separated the front of the building from the newsroom. Behind the counter, several people were sitting at desks, working at computers, cutting and pasting news stories and pictures onto the page-layout matrix that was on the screen in front of them. John, who had come to the newspaper office alone, stepped up to the counter. He stood there for a moment until a young woman noticed him.

"May I be of some assistance?" she asked.

"Yes. I would like to speak to Esteban Cortina."

"One moment, please."

John watched the young woman walk to one of the desks near the back where a man was staring at a monitor while moving a mouse around. She leaned down to say something to him. He looked up toward the front at John, then stood up. He was tall and well built, clean shaven, and, John would guess, in his late thirties or early forties.

"*Qué?*" he asked when he approached the counter.

"Senor Cortina, I am a reporter for the *Mobile Reg-*

ister. I wish to do a story about the music of Colombia. I hear that you can tell me many delightful tales."

Cortina nodded. "I once visited Mobile. It is a beautiful place."

Good, John thought. All was going according to plan, in that the man had responded properly to the password challenge. Of course, since the operation had been compromised, the response was no longer the guarantee it once was.

"Come," Cortina said. "There is a better place to talk."

John followed Cortina through a door and down a long, narrow hallway. He was aware of the presence of a Glock 33 .357 magnum in his pocket, and he put his hand on the small but very powerful pistol, to be ready, just in case.

Cortina led him out of the hallway into the press room. Here, eight huge web presses were online, most of them running.

A loud bell rang on the press nearest them, then it began to rumble and roar as it started, adding to the bedlam of seven other operating presses. Within seconds, newsprint was flying through all the components of the press, starting out from a huge white row, and ending up as printed and folded material.

"Is your entire team here?" Cortina asked, the ambient noise so loud that John could barely hear him. He understood then why Cortina was so careful about bringing him back here. If John had been wearing a wire, it would be useless because of all the noise.

"Yes," John said. "We are in place."

"Do you have vehicles fit for travel?"

"Yes. And weapons." John was going out on a limb now, telling him about the vehicles and weapons, but he had a gut feeling that Cortina was just who he claimed to be.

"Good. Be in front of the Dugger's and Green Hotel at four o'clock in the morning," Cortina ordered. "I will meet you there and lead you to the field headquarters to meet the commander of the resistance."

"We will be there," John promised.

Jose Arino and Simone Ortega were dressed all in black so that, even though they were walking around on the roof of the Hotel Intercontinental, they blended into the black of the night sky. As a result, nobody saw Jose step to the edge of the building, then turn around.

One end of a rope was wrapped several times around a flagpole, while Jose held the other end in the rappel position.

"Hold the rope until I reach the window," Jose ordered.

"*Sí,*" Simone replied. Since it was wrapped around the flagpole, none of Jose's weight would be on Simone. All he had to do was keep the rope from coming loose.

The hotel was only eight floors high, and the window Jose was going to was on the eighth floor. He pushed himself off, rappelled down the rope, then stopped just in front of the window. Looking into the room, he saw nothing. He hung on to the rope with one hand while, with the other, he pushed the window up. After that, he let himself into the room.

Jose could hear the hair-dryer going in the bathroom. Noticing that a lamp was turned on by the bed, he snapped it off, then moved into the shadows of the corner to wait.

When Linda stepped out of the shower, she dried off, then wrapped the towel around herself and began drying her hair. Her hair was long and luxuriously black, and though she knew that it probably should be much shorter, considering the situations she often got herself into, she was reluctant to cut it. Besides, when she stopped to think about it, her long hair had come in handy many times, helping her to pass herself off in one guise or another.

After ten minutes of drying, Linda turned off the dryer and stepped out of the bathroom. From the moment she was outside the bathroom she was on alert. She was certain that she had left a small bedside lamp on, but the room was dark. Not only that, she felt a tingling sensation . . . as if someone was in the room.

Poised for anything, she turned on a light. That was when a man, dressed in black, stepped out from the far corner of the room.

"Who are you?" Linda asked. Her question was amazingly calm under the circumstances.

"My name is Jose," the man replied.

"Well, Jose, the next question is, what are you doing in my room?"

Jose was holding a gun and he raised it to make certain she saw it. "You are to come with me," he said.

Linda stepped up close to him, then smiled at him.

"Honey, if you're here to rape me, we don't have to go anywhere," she said. "We can do anything you want, right here."

"I'm not—" the intruder started to say, but Linda interrupted him.

"I like sex as much as anyone," she said. She undid the towel and let it drop.

Jose, seeing Linda's beautiful, naked form, drew in a quick breath of surprise and appreciation. As she knew he would, he took his eyes off her face and concentrated on her obvious charms. He lowered the gun slightly.

That was exactly the opening Linda was looking for and she snatched the pistol from his hand. In the same motion, she spun around on her left foot and, with her right foot, sent a smashing blow into Jose's throat, crushing his larynx.

Jose put both hands to his throat and took a few steps back, struggling to breathe. Linda spun around again and kicked him a second time, this time with the bottom of her foot. This kick drove Jose back through the same open window he had used to gain access to the room.

As Jose went out he made a desperate grab, first for the windowsill, then for the rope he had used to rappel down on. He missed both opportunities, then, with his eyes open wide in fear, he felt himself going through. Jose opened his mouth to scream but the crushed larynx prevented any sound. Linda moved quickly to the window and saw him flailing his arms as he fell, then she heard the splat as he hit the asphalt of the parking lot, eight floors below. He didn't make a move after that.

Up on the roof, Simone had also seen Jose come flying through the window and he watched, help-lessly, as his friend flailed at the air while falling to his death below.

Frightened that he might have been seen, or that someone might know that he was here, Simone stepped back, quickly, from the edge of the roof.

This had not gone well tonight. They were told that all they had to do was kill a defenseless woman, then collect one thousand dollars. Simone came to the conclusion that either there was someone in there with her or she obviously wasn't the defense-less woman they were led to believe that she was.

Whatever it was, he didn't plan to stick around long enough to find out.

Fifteen minutes later, Linda met Chris in the bar downstairs. Outside she could hear the sirens of the approaching ambulance and police cars, and several in the bar were standing by the windows, looking outside at the flashing red and blue lights.

"You missed all the excitement," Chris said when Linda joined him at his table.

"Not all of it."

"What do you mean not—" Chris started to say, then stopped in midsentence. "I'll be damned. You?"

"Let's just say I didn't sign up for a roommate."

"How did he get in?"

"The window was open."

"Then he was no ordinary burglar or mugger. First they went after Jennifer, now you. They seem to be going after the women."

"It looks that way," Linda said. "But a more serious question is, how do they know who and where we are? How are they getting their information?"

"Beats the hell out of me," Chris said. He chuckled. "What is it?"

"Whoever is providing the information doesn't know everything. He sure was wrong in thinking you might be an easy target."

National Television System studios, New York

"Stand by for down-line commercials," the floor director called. He held his hand up. "Live in five, four, three, two, one! Intro rolling!"

Music came up, and a spinning box in the middle

of the screen grew larger until it stopped. The box said REPORT TO THE NATION. The box went away to be replaced by a darkened set, showing two people in silhouette.

A deep, mellow voice-over intoned the intro.

"Report to the nation, with Jim Williams. Today's guest, Luiz Alberto Mendoza, president designate of the new nation of Pangea. And now, here is Jim Williams."

The lights came up and the camera moved in for a one-shot of Jim Williams. Jim, a rather round-faced, blue-eyed man with light brown hair, stared intently at the camera.

"It isn't often that a new nation is carved out of an existing country without going through the trauma of a civil war. But apparently that is the case in the South American country of Colombia, for if all goes to plan, in just under two months from now, the new nation of Pangea will be born.

"With me today is Luiz Alberto Mendoza, the man who will be president of this new nation."

The camera moved out for a two-shot.

"Mr. Mendoza, welcome to the show."

"Thank you for having me, Mr. Williams."

"Carving a new nation from an existing country, without having to fight a civil war, is something that is almost unheard of. How did this come about?"

"I think it became evident to the government in Bogata that Colombia was becoming increasingly polarized, that people from Medellin to Cali to Mocoa had interests totally different from the rest of the country."

"Your critics agree with you, but say that those different interests include the manufacture and distribution of drugs."

"I will not lie to you," Mendoza said. "We do have

that reputation. But it is something that I will deal with."

"Are you saying that you are going to eliminate all drug production in your new country?"

"No, I'm not saying that. Indeed, I don't think it can be eliminated . . . it is too deeply entrenched in our culture, and too many of our citizens depend upon this for their livelihood, not only those who grow it, but those who work in the growing, processing, packaging, and distribution of the product."

"It isn't product, it is dope."

"Yes, dope. And like I said, I will deal with it."

"How will you deal with it?"

"I will control it, regulate it. You know, not all drug production is bad. Some drugs serve noble purposes as medicines . . . and other drugs lend themselves to experimentation for new cures. Would it not be wonderful if, in our controlled drug industry, we discovered a cure for cancer?"

"That would be good, of course, but in the meantime we have the other problem to worry about, the cocaine, heroin, the drugs that appear on the streets in the U.S. I'm sure you agree with me that these drugs are dangerous and cause innumerable problems."

"Yes," Mendoza agreed. "That is a bad thing." He held up his finger. "But that is the problem of the U.S., not Pangea. It is up to the U.S. to decrease the demand for these drugs. I have nothing to do with enforcing the laws of the United States, nor would anyone in American want me to."

"But you can see, can't you, that making the drugs so readily available just exacerbates the problem?"

Mendoza shook his head. "As I said, the ultimate solution has to lie within the borders of the United States itself. Americans must regulate themselves;

they must control their appetite and thus remove the market. If there was no market for the drugs, then we would not be able to sell them. In the meantime, my hands are tied. You must understand that drug trafficking, legal and illegal, is our biggest source of revenue. What kind of president would I be for our country if I attempted to stop the main source of income for our people? And, in Pangea at least, I intend to make it legal."

"Yes, well, let's move on, shall we?" Williams said. "You are the president designate. What type of government will Pangea have?"

"I will establish a parliament," Mendoza said. "The people will vote for representatives within that parliament, and the parliament will be authorized to make proposals and to advise me on affairs of state."

"Will they be able to pass laws?"

"Yes, of course, subject to my approval."

"Your approval?"

"Is it not so in your own country? Does the president not have the authority to veto a bill that he does not want passed?"

"Yes, but the veto can be overridden by a two-thirds majority of the House and Senate. Can your veto be overridden?"

"No, I think such bickering between the legislative and executive branch can only create chaos."

"I see. What about elections for president?"

Mendoza shook his head. "No elections are needed. It is my country, I conceived of the idea, and I convinced the government in Bogota to grant us our independence. I don't think anyone else understands my vision for us, or has my determination to make this new country work. Therefore, I have taken to myself the position of el presidente for life."

"Before we finish with this segment, is there any-

thing you would like to say to the American people?"
Williams asked.

"Yes," Mendoza said. "Not to the American people,
but to the American government." Mendoza stared
at the camera, then, raising his finger, he began
speaking in an authoritative tone.

"Mr. President, I know that you have sent some of
your operatives down to my country to try and desta-
bilize us. I am here to tell you, right now, that we
know they are there, we even know who and where
they are.

"By engaging in such activity, you are violating international law by invading a sovereign country. But
I tell you this, Mr. President. We will find them, we
will kill them, and we will send them back to you in
body bags."

The White House

The president of the United States was watching
the show, and when Mendoza issued his closing challenge, the president picked up the phone and dialed
a number. After a moment, the head of the CIA
came on the line.

"Yes, Mr. President?"

"Were you watching *Report to the Nation?*"

"I was."

"Is Mendoza right? Do we have a team operating
in Colombia right now?"

"No, Mr. President, we do not."

"What about DEA, FBI? What about the military?
Do any of them have people down there?"

"No, sir," the director answered. "I have checked
thoroughly. We have no one down there from the
government."

"From the government?" the president said, quickly picking up on the slight nuance of the director's response.

"Yes, sir," the director replied. "From the government." The director made no further explanation, nor did the president ask for it.

"Very well. Thank you, Mr. Director," the president said.

Chapter 8

Parking lot of Dugger's and Green Hotel,
Cali, Colombia

"What time is it?" Linda asked.

Paul pushed a button on his watch and, by the tiny glow it caused, checked the time.

"It's about five minutes until four," he said. As he released the button, the inside of the HumVee was dark again.

Paul, Linda, Mike, and Don Yee were in this HumVee. John, Jennifer, and Chris were in the one right beside them. The two HumVees were sitting in the parking lot in front of the Dugger's and Green Hotel, positioned in a way that would give them a clear view of the front of the hotel.

The windows were down and they could hear the serenade of the night creatures. Nearby was the gentle whisper of an operating sprinkler, and the predawn darkness was heavy with the sweet fragrance of flowers.

"You think our man will show?" Mike asked.

"No reason to expect that he should," Paul replied. "Nothing seems to be going right, so far."

"Wait a minute," Don said, pointing. "What's that?"

A taxi turned off the main road, then drove up the long driveway to the front of the hotel.

"I don't know," Linda said. "But I have a feeling this is the guy we're waiting for."

"Have you ever seen him?" Paul asked.

"No. But who else would arrive at exactly four in the morning?"

In the HumVee next to them, John also saw the cab arrive.

"That's him. That's Cortina," he said when he saw the passenger step out of the cab.

"What now?" Jennifer asked.

"Wait until the cab drives away," John said.

Even as John was answering Jennifer, the cab turned around and started back up the long driveway, leaving Cortina standing in front of the hotel.

John dialed a number, and all watched as Cortina took his cell phone from his shirt pocket.

"*Si?*"

"Look to your right," John said.

John pulled the turn signal lever and the lights flashed once, then went dark again.

"I see it."

John turned off his cell phone and watched as Cortina walked across the entry drive and came into the parking lot. John had the switch set so that the light wouldn't come on when the vehicle door was opened. Cortina got in.

"Esteban Cortina, this is Jennifer Barns and Chris Farmer. I'll introduce the others when we get to where we are going. We are going somewhere, aren't we?"

"Yes," Esteban answered. "Turn right as soon as you exit the parking lot."

John started his vehicle, which was a signal to the others to start theirs as well. He followed Esteban's directions out of the parking lot, with Mike driving the other HumVee behind him.

There was very little traffic on the streets at this

time of morning, so they moved through the town quickly, then took a road marked A BUENAVENTURA.

"Are we going to Buenaventura?" John asked.

"Not all the way," Esteban replied.

Within a few miles after leaving town they turned off the main, paved road, then continued on along a smaller road that was sometimes dirt and sometimes gravel. The road began to climb higher and higher as they started across the Andes Mountains.

By midmorning the road had grown very muddy and was quite bad. At about noon, they arrived at a small town that wasn't even on the map.

"What is this place?" John asked.

"It is called Pueblo de Agua Buena, the Town of Good Water," Cortena said.

It was as if the town were from another time, far away from the trials and tribulations of the rest of the world, or even Colombia. There was an equilateral plaza in town and one side was occupied by the cathedral. The other three sides were lined by cafés, cantinas, ice-cream shops, and a shop for farming tools.

The people of the town looked like something from a travel brochure, wearing ponchos, sombreros, and knives hanging from their belts.

The Code Name Team took their lunch in one of the sidewalk cafés and watched a large burial procession leave from the cathedral.

"The people here are good people," Esteban said. "They know of the drug trafficking, but they do not take part in it."

They were quiet for a moment, then Esteban continued. "It is from towns like this that my uncle will draw the army he needs to fight Mendoza." He had a very serious expression on his face. Then, suddenly, he broke into a wide grin. "And it is friends like you who will help us," he said.

They continued their trip after lunch, and when they reached the top of the pass, they encountered a very deep chasm, over which stretched a suspension bridge. John stopped and got out. Mike, who was driving the HumVee behind him, got out as well. The two men, plus Esteban, walked up to the edge of the bridge.

The bridge was about fifty yards long, and the chasm it crossed was at least a thousand feet deep. As they stood there looking out over the deep arroyo, a flight of vultures began circling overhead. Paul pointed to them.

"Do they know something we don't know?" he asked. John chuckled, then bent over to examine the structure of the bridge.

"The bridge is safe," Esteban said. "We have used it many times."

"What were you in when you crossed?"

"A jeep, most of the time. Sometimes a pickup truck," Esteban said.

John pointed to the HumVees. "These things weigh a lot more than a jeep, or a pickup truck, especially with the armor plating."

"And don't forget the weapons," Mike added.

John examined the bridge again. It was suspended from four large steel cables. A network of smaller cables held the bridge floor to the larger cables. The bridge floor was made up of two-by-four wooden planks, connected by tie bars.

"All right," John said. "Here is what we'll do. We'll get all our people out, then I'll drive across first. Mike, if I make it, you come next."

"Should we send our people across on foot first?" Mike asked.

"Yes," John said. Then, after a second, he changed his mind. "No," he said quickly. "If they get over there and one of us takes the bridge down, they'll be trapped on the other side."

Mike chuckled. "And if I'm the one falling a thousand feet, I'll think about them being trapped as I'm on my way down."

John laughed as well. "You are nothing if you aren't a thoughtful man," he said. "All right, let's get it done."

"What about the weapons?"

"What about them?"

"Should we off-load them as well?"

John thought for a moment, then he shook his head. "No, we'll leave the weapons in the vehicles."

"Whatever you say."

"Look, if you'd rather, I'll drive across, then come back and drive yours across," John offered.

Mike held up his hands, palms out. "No need for that, I'll drive it. Uh, you are going first, aren't you?"

"I'll go first," John agreed.

"Good. I figure if you can make it, I can."

John, Mike, and Esteban returned to the two vehicles to give the others word on what they were about to do.

"I've examined the bridge very closely," John said, "and I'm pretty sure it will hold us."

"You're 'pretty' sure?" Jennifer asked, emphasizing the word.

"Yes, well, we'll see, won't we?" John replied gamely. He got into the first HumVee, started it, then drove it to the near edge of the bridge. Then, very slowly, he started out onto it.

The bridge creaked and groaned as the heavy HumVee pulled onto it. One of the smaller cables, supporting the flooring, snapped, with a loud twang.

"John, be careful!" Jennifer called.

John stopped, then proceeded on, barely moving.

Everyone watched, holding their breath, until he was on the other side. Then, when he pulled off the bridge, all cheered.

"All right, Mike, it's your turn," Linda said.

"Uh, yeah," Mike replied.

Mike pulled onto the bridge then, and again everyone held their breath. About halfway across the bridge, several of the smaller cables popped and snapped. John, who was standing on the other side, waved his arm.

"Mike, come on, gun it across!" he shouted.

Mike floored the accelerator and the HumVee leaped forward. He sped across the bridge with nearly a dozen of the smaller cables snapping behind him. By the time he got across, the suspension bridge was hanging low on one side, where most of the smaller support cables had broken.

"Let's go," Chris said.

"All of us? At the same time?" Paul asked.

"All of us together don't weigh as much as one of the vehicles. And with the bridge hanging down on one side, we can help each other across, if need be."

Chris led them out onto the bridge. When they got to the part where all of the cables on one side were broken, the flooring was so unstable that it tilted sharply and Chris fell.

"Chris!" Linda shouted as Chris hit the floor, then slid off. Paul, who was right behind him, dropped to the floor and reached out to grab Chris by the wrist.

For a long moment Paul lay there, holding on to Chris's wrist, suspending him over the one-thousand-foot drop.

"Don, grab hold of my legs!" Paul called. "I'm being dragged off here."

Don and Esteban both grabbed hold of Paul's legs.

They heard someone running toward them and, looking up, saw Mike coming.

"Hang on, Chris, we'll get you up," Paul said.

"I don't have plans to go anywhere," Chris replied, his voice amazingly calm.

When Mike got to the place where the floor was badly tilted, he got down on his hands and knees and crawled across. Then, lying down beside Paul, he reached down.

"Give me your other hand," Mike said.

Chris tried to reach up, but couldn't get his other hand high enough for Mike to reach him.

"Pull him up a little, Paul," Chris said.

"I don't know that I can," Paul said, his voice strained. "I don't have that good of a hold and if I try to improve it, I might drop him."

"Linda, you and Jennifer hold Paul's leg here," Don said. "Let me see what I can do.

Linda and Jennifer grabbed Mike's right leg, while Esteban continued to hang on to his left.

Don was not very large, but for now that worked to his advantage, because he crawled over the top of Mike, then reached down over Paul's hand and wrapped his hand around Chris's wrist.

"Come on, Paul, let's both of us pull," Don said. "We can do it."

With both of them straining, they managed to lift Chris up just a little, but that was far enough for Mike to get hold of him.

"Grab my wrist, Chris," Mike said, as he wrapped his fingers in a death grip around Chris's wrist.

Chris was a big man, but with Mike, Don, and Paul all three pulling, they managed to haul him rather easily back up onto the bridge.

Chris and Paul lay there for a moment as they

caught their breath, for they were the two who had expended the most energy.

"Let's get on across this damn thing," Chris finally said.

"I suggest we crawl until we get back over to where the bridge is square again," Paul said.

"Good idea," Mike agreed.

The two women went first, followed by Esteban, then Don, then Mike, then Chris, and finally Paul. John met them when they finally reached the other side.

"What the hell kept you?" John asked.

"My fault, Chief," Chris replied. "I thought I would just . . . hang around . . . for a while to get a better look at the scenery."

The others laughed uproariously. It wasn't really all that funny, but it was just what was needed to break the somber mood.

Chapter 9

Southwest Colombia

It had been at least five miles since they left the road. They were driving now along a dry streambed and it was nearly dark when Esteban held up his hand as a signal for John to stop.

"We're here," he said.

"Neat," Jennifer said. She extended her lower lip and blew an errant strand of hair back from her forehead. "Just where is here?"

Esteban stepped out of the HumVee, then cupped his hands around his mouth and let out a long, piercing yell.

"Eeeeeyot!"

Esteban's shout echoed back from the hills. He waited until all the echoes died, then shouted again.

"Eeeeeeyot!"

Again the echoes returned. Then, a few seconds after the final echo, they heard a return shout.

"Eeeeyot!"

Esteban smiled. "Okay," he said. "Let's go."

"Go where?"

"There," Esteban said, pointing to a large bush. Even as he pointed, the bush began moving, opening up a small road.

John and the others got back into their vehicles,

then drove through the opening made by the moving bush. To John's pleasant surprise, the road on the other side of the bush was much easier driving than had been the dry streambed.

John followed the road for about half a mile.

"John," Jennifer said, pointing.

"Yes, I see him," John said. "There is another."

John and Jennifer were pointing out armed guards who, while making no effort to stop them, were following them closely with their eyes.

At the end, the road made a sharp turn to the left and there, hidden under overhanging tree branches, was a camp. It could almost be called a village, for the buildings were actually quite well constructed.

There were two parallel rows of buildings, running east and west on the south side of the camp, and two more parallel rows running east and west on the north side of the camp. The camp was protected, north and south, by sheer-faced cliffs. A huge chasm protected the west end of the camp, so that the only entrance was from the east.

The middle of the camp was an open area, rather like a parade ground. That illusion was further heightened by the fact that there was a flagpole in the middle, surrounded by a circle of white rocks. The flag of Colombia flew from the top of the pole. A couple of pickup trucks and three jeeps were parked under a flagpole.

In addition to the many armed men milling around, there were also women and children. And some of the women were armed.

"Esteban!" a gray-haired man said, coming to greet him. The two men embraced.

"This is my uncle Ricardo," Esteban said. "He is the leader of our movement, *Libere Brigada de Colom-*

bia. Uncle, this is John Barrone. He and his friends have come to help us."

"From *Estados Unidos?*" Ricardo asked, his face showing his pleasure.

John paused for a second, then nodded. "Yes," he said.

"Good, good. I did not think the United States would wish Mendoza to succeed in creating a country based upon drugs. Welcome, my friends. Welcome to Camp Bolivar."

Several of the residents of the camp came to greet the visitors, including many women and a surprising number of children.

"I would not have thought there would be so many children here," Jennifer said, as she smiled at one of the little girls.

"Some of our people fear that their loved ones will be kidnapped if they leave them in town," Ricardo said. "So they have brought them to the camp. We welcome them. It makes this place more like a home to us."

"Senor Cortina. What sort of popular support does the Free Colombia Brigade enjoy?" John asked Ricardo.

"The . . ." Ricardo started to answer, then looked at his nephew for translation. "*Promedio?*"

"Average," Esteban said.

"*Sí.* The average Colombian supports us." Ricardo pointed to the men and women walking around in the camp. "These are average Colombians," he said.

"What sort of weapons do you have?" Chris asked.

"I will show you," Ricardo said. He shouted to one of the other men, and when the man came over, Ricardo said, "Have all turn out with their weapons for an inspection."

"*Sí, Comandante.*"

"That is Miguel Martinez," Ricardo said. "He is third in command."

"Third?"

"My nephew, Esteban, is second in command," Ricardo said. He sighed. "I do not know if he is the best military person I have, but I do know that I can trust him with my life."

"Under the circumstances, making him your number two seems like a smart idea," John said.

Miguel began shouting orders to the others, and there was a furry of activity as everyone scrambled to comply. Within two minutes, the entire camp was turned out and standing in formation. All of them were holding weapons.

"Any crew-served weapons?" John asked.

"*Qué?*"

"I mean heavy weapons, like machine guns?"

Ricardo shook his head. "No."

"Well then, we'll just have to correct that, won't we?" John said. He pointed to the two HumVees.

"You have such weapons?" Ricardo asked, excitedly.

"We do. Chris, show our friends what we have."

Chris began taking some of the weapons from the HumVees and laying them out on the ground. The men of the little village gathered around in excitement as Chris held up each weapon and explained it to them.

"Have you had any military operations yet?" John asked.

"We've attacked a few of their roadblocks," Ricardo said. "That's all."

"I've been telling my uncle that we need to do something that will let the people know we are fighting for them," Esteban.

"We will, we will," Ricardo said. "As soon as the right opportunity comes along."

"What do you say that we prepare for that opportunity by getting in a little training?" John asked.

"Training?"

"Give us two weeks to work with your men," John suggested. "We'll teach them how to use the new weapons, and how to work together."

"*Maravilloso. Magnífico,*" Ricardo said, clapping enthusiastically.

"Hello, John," a female voice said.

Looking into the crowd of people who had gathered around the jeep, John recognized Katy Correal.

"Katy," he said in surprise. "You're here?"

"Welcome," she said. "Come, let me show you around." She took his arm and led him away from the others.

"You look surprised to see me here," Katy said with a little laugh.

"Well, yes, I am," John replied. "The other day, when we were talking, you didn't seem to know much about the Free Colombia Brigade."

"No," Katy replied. "What I didn't know much about was you. I could not take a chance on speaking out of turn, and perhaps endangering my friends."

"Then you did know what Brian was really doing down here?"

"Yes, of course. We were working together," Katy said. She held up her finger. "But I wasn't the only one who was not telling the whole truth. You aren't a detective looking into what happened to Brian, are you?"

"No. I'm here to help the folks who want to keep Colombia as one country."

"Are you with the CIA?"

"No."

"FBI?"

"I'm not with the government," John said.

"Oh, that is too bad."

"Why too bad?"

"Because if we had the United States Government behind us, we could not lose. But you are just mercenaries."

"You might call us that," John said. "But I know that we have the tacit, if not specific, approval of the U.S. Government."

"How do you know that?"

"Well, it's no secret that the U.S. does not want Pangea to break away from Colombia. They have said as much on several occasions. Therefore, anyone who is fighting against the secession will enjoy the moral, if not the physical, support of the U.S. Government."

"Moral support," Katy said. "Ha! A lot of good moral support will do us. We need more than that."

"Exactly," John said. "My group and I are giving you more than moral support."

"Yes, you are," Katy agreed. "And I apologize for not showing more gratitude. Well, here we are," she said, taking in the village with a wave of her hand. "This is our living area. As you can see, those with families have their own, private quarters. The rest of us, those of us who are single, live in these two long huts. This one is for the men," she said, pointing to the one on the right. "And this one is for the women."

"Live here? You mean, you've given up your job with the Ministry of Agriculture?"

"Yes," Katy said. "After you came to see me the other day, I began to get worried. I didn't know who you were, but your questions were getting too close, so I thought it might be best to leave while I could."

"I'm sorry I frightened you, and I'm sorry if I caused you to lose your job."

"Well, if this Pangea thing goes through, I would lose my job anyway," Katy said. "So I may as well try and do something about it. Besides, I feel like I owe it to Brian."

"I'm sure Brian would appreciate that," John said.

Katy looked at her watch. "Oh, it's time for dinner," she said. "You'll be eating in the community dining room with the rest of us, I hope."

"Well, we have MREs," John said. "I would hate to take any of your food."

"Nonsense, you are bringing weapons and ammunition," Katy said. "The least we can do is feed you, and I'm certain Ricardo would insist that you eat with us. Besides, it has to be better than MREs, whatever those things are," she added, wrinkling her nose.

"Then, on behalf of the others, we accept your invitation," John said.

The Russell Senate Office Building,
Washington, D.C.

Senator Josh Fitzgerald Kelly wadded the sheet of paper into a ball, then aimed it toward the wastebasket. It bounced off the rim of the basket and lay on the floor alongside.

On the wall behind Kelly was a framed set of medals he had won while serving in Vietnam. The medals, displayed on a background of black velvet, consisted of a Purple Heart, a Bronze Star, and an Air Medal, along with the normal awards given to all who had served in Vietnam.

Kelly had been an army personnel officer in the United States Army, Vietnam, serving his entire tour of duty at the USARV Headquarters in Saigon. One night while enjoying coq au vin at the My Kahn Floating Restaurant, a bomb went off just inside the entrance. Kelly and his date, a young Vietnamese woman who worked at the offices of USARV, were on the far side of the restaurant, and out of the direct effect of the blast. However, a waiter just happened to be passing their table when the bomb went off, and he dropped a water pitcher. The water pitcher shattered, and Kelly was cut by pieces of flying glass. The glass left two gashes on his arm, one barely a scratch, and one that bled enough to stain his jungle fatigues.

Kelly left the restaurant as soon as he could and reported directly to First Field Hospital, just across from Tan San Nhut. The doctor on duty took a look at it, probed around a bit to see if there was anything in the wound, then, deciding that it was free of any pieces of glass, cleaned it with hydrogen peroxide and treated it with iodine. After that he made a small patch of gauze and taped it over the cut.

"There you go, Lieutenant," the doctor said. "You are as good as new."

"Is that it? Is that all there is to it?" Kelly asked.

The doctor chuckled. "That's it. What did you expect, amputation?"

"No, but this was a combat injury."

"Combat? I thought you said you were hit with a piece of flying glass."

"I think it was glass, but whatever it was, it was the result of a bomb blast down at the My Khan. So, that means I was wounded by direct enemy action."

"Wait a minute," the doctor, an army major, said. "Don't tell me you're asking me to authorize a Purple Heart?"

"Why not? I've earned one."

The smile left the doctor's face, and he pointed toward the hospital ward behind him.

"Lieutenant, I've got kids in there who have lost arms, legs, peckers, even. Dustoff brought two men in today who died on the operating tables. Those men earned Purple Hearts. Now, do you intend to stand there and say that for this scratch you want a Purple Heart?"

"I was wounded as a direct result of enemy action," Kelly said. "That means I have earned a Purple Heart."

The doctor glared at him for a moment longer, then jerking open a drawer, ripped out a DD-95 and filled it out, recommending Kelly for the Purple Heart.

"Take it, you arrogant, selfish, strap-hanging son of a bitch. And I hope it shames you every time you wear it."

The next step would be for it to go through personnel. That step was automatic, because all that was required to qualify was a doctor's certificate that the wound was as a direct result of enemy action. Ironically, Kelly himself would handle that stage.

The Air Medal was almost as contrived as the Purple Heart. All he needed to get the Air Medal was fifty hours of Direct Combat Support flying. Kelly scheduled himself for enough routine flights to Vung Tau, Ben Hoa, Long Binh, and Phu Loi to make sure he got the hours he needed. Once he was qualified, he put himself in for, and was awarded, the Air Medal.

The Bronze Star was not for bravery, but for service, and was awarded to virtually every officer who served a tour of duty in Vietnam. The thing about the Bronze Star was that it sounded so much more important than it really was.

When he returned from his tour in Vietnam,

Kelly decided to run for the U.S Congress. To his chagrin, dissatisfaction with the war in Vietnam had reached its peak, so the medals and his service in Vietnam, rather than benefiting him, actually hurt him. Deciding to take a different route, Kelly joined the Vietnam Veterans' Peace Now Committee and, wearing his fatigues, participated in VVPN protests during which he and the other marchers (many of whom were not actually Vietnam veterans) were carrying VC flags and antiwar signs. Kelly assumed the persona of the soul-scarred Vietnam veteran, struggling to live with the terrible atrocities he and the other American soldiers had committed.

In a highly publicized act, he threw his ribbons (but kept the medals) over the front gate at the White House. He also testified before the House Armed Services Committee, during which time he confessed to being a party to atrocities committed "in the name of U.S. arrogance."

That bit of showboating got him elected to Congress in the next election, and to the Senate two years after that.

Now, however, it was once again politically advantageous to tout his wartime service. Josh Fitzgerald Kelly, whose most dangerous activity was riding through the streets of Saigon in a cyclo, was widely regarded by his supporters as a war hero.

Carl Mobley, his administrative assistant, stepped into his office then and, leaning down, picked up the wad of paper and tossed it into the wastebasket.

"Two points," he said.

"Maybe so, but I'm credited with the assist," Kelly said. "What's up?"

"Luiz Mendoza," Carl replied.

"Mendoza? Who is Luiz Mendoza?"

"He is the president designate of Pangea," Carl said.

"Oh yeah," Kelly replied. "He's the guy who is trying to start a new country, right? And he has asked for U.S. recognition? Ha. What an asshole."

"Maybe not so much of an asshole," Carl replied.

"Why? What do you mean?"

"He has already picked up the support of France, Germany, Algeria, and Cuba. France is going to propose Pangea for membership in the United Nations."

"Yeah, but that's going nowhere, and you know it."

"That doesn't mean we can't find some advantage from it."

"How so?"

"If you would propose a bill before the Senate, granting recognition, it would be worth five million dollars," Carl said.

"Five million dollars?" Kelly whistled lightly. "That's a lot of money," he said. "But how would we do it? I can't accept money for a bill proposal. That would open me up to a charge of graft."

"The five million dollars would go to a political action committee," Carl explained, "one that you control. You could then give the money to other senators and congressmen as they needed it for their own reelections. Think of what a tremendous power base that would give you, to have all those senators and congressmen beholding to you."

"Yeah," Kelly said. He began stroking his rather long chin as he contemplated the suggestion. "Yeah, and not only that, if we granted them recognition, it would give us some voice in their new government. We could use that voice to fight against further drug dealing."

"Precisely. Which we cannot do if we don't grant them recognition. Let's face it, Senator," Carl said, on a roll now as he began composing Senator Kelly's speech. "If we do not recognize them, we will be deaf, dumb, and blind in the new government. That would be the worst thing we could do in this atmosphere."

"All right, so what do we do next?" Kelly asked.

"With your permission, I'll make contact with Mendoza . . . I'll tell him what we want for your support, then I'll set up a meeting for you."

"I don't want to meet here," Kelly said.

"No, not here," Carl replied. "I'll find a place, perhaps outside of Washington. What about New York? You're speaking to the Friends of the Environment there in a couple of days. I could set up a meeting somewhere in New York."

"Sounds good," Kelly said. "Do it."

New York, New York

Mendoza was in a suite at the Algonquin Hotel in New York. He had already been on two nationally televised talk shows, and he had met with several United Nations delegations, lobbying for their support. Everyone knew how much money the drug trafficking generated, and the promise of shared wealth had been very effective in winning support.

He was going over his schedule for the next several days when the phone rang. His adjutant, Gato Valdez, answered the phone.

"*Sí,*" he said.

Gato listened for a moment, then covered the mouthpiece with his hand. "El Presidente, Senator Kelly wants to come to New York to meet with you."

"Why?"

"He says it is for a mutual advantage."

Mendoza started toward the phone, then stopped. "Is that the senator on the phone now?"

"No, El Presidente, it is his administrative assistant."

"I am a president," Mendoza said. "I do not talk to administrative assistants. You handle it."

"*Si*," Gato said.

Chapter 10

Camp Bolivar

A powerful mine exploding just in front and slightly to the left of Linda caused her ears to ring and flashed its heat against her face. Mud, water, tiny shards of gravel, and burning bits of guncotton rained down on her as smoke from the blast drifted off through the gray, rain-washed air. Just inches above her, machine-gun bullets cracked loudly in their deadly transit.

Linda looked at the others. They were wriggling on their bellies through explosive charges, maneuvering across a machine-gun-raked, muddy field, sliding under concertina wire, rolling over logs, and trying to maintain their weapons in firing condition while keeping themselves below the kill zone. When she looked toward the far side of the field she could see the two machine guns at the objective, squirting out gleaming beads of tracer rounds to flash just overhead.

Linda flinched at another, very close explosion, barely cognizant of the liquid mud that oozed down over her ears, matting her hair and sliding under her shirt. She was totally covered with the stuff. She took a deep breath, made several more snakelike lunges forward, then clambered over the last berm.

"Up here, up here!" someone was shouting. Checking the machine guns, Linda saw that her last rush forward had carried her far enough beyond them to take her out of their field of fire. Instead, the bullets were whipping across those few unfortunate souls who were still mired in the mud of the open field. Linda stood up and, holding her rifle at high port, ran as fast as she could at a crouch toward the point at which they were to rendezvous. Reaching her goal, she belly-flopped down onto the wet grass, while behind her the machine guns maintained their staccato firing, interspersed with the steady thump of explosions.

"Cease fire, cease fire!"

Abruptly, the guns and the explosions stilled. For a long, breathless moment, there was dead quiet . . . an unearthly quiet when contrasted to the din of just a few seconds earlier

"You did well, Linda," Jennifer said.

Linda rolled over onto her back and lay there for a moment, looking up at Jennifer, who was smiling down at her. "Yeah, well, why me?" she asked.

"Somebody had to go through the training cycle with them," John said.

"What about Mike or Chris, or Don? No, never mind Don, he would never have made it."

"We needed a woman," John said, coming over to join them. "Machismo is important to these men. And if they see a woman going through it, they wouldn't dare say they couldn't do it."

"And I couldn't do it, I had to set all the explosives," Jennifer said sweetly. "Anyway, it wasn't all that bad, was it?"

"Oh no," Linda replied. "I enjoy having mud oozing through the crack of my ass."

Esteban came over then. Like Linda, Esteban had

made the training exercise and, like her, he was covered with mud.

"Oh, that was great fun!" he said. "You are very good, Senorita Linda. I tried hard to beat you, but couldn't."

"*Caramba, Pienso que ella es* Wonder Woman!" one of the other men said.

Linda chuckled. "Yeah, I'm Wonder Woman, all right. I'm all dressed up for the ball."

"I've got a shower set up for you," Chris said.

"Thanks."

"Want me to wash your back? Get that nasty old mud out of the crack of your ass?"

"No, thanks."

"Just checking," Chris said with a smile.

"Linda," John called as Linda started toward the shower. She stopped and looked back at him.

"Don't forget . . . briefing at 1900."

"Got ya," Linda said with a little wave.

Chris pointed out the shower. It was a canvas screen that covered just enough of her to provide for some degree of privacy. The water came through a long hose that stretched across an open field, then up the side of a mountain where it was fed by a springhead. The water that was in the part of the hose exposed to the sun was warm, but once that water ran out, the water from the creek was cold.

Linda stayed under the water a little too long, enjoying the warm spray, only to have it interrupted by the sudden change in temperature when she was hit by the cold spring water. But after a moment of adjustment, she found even that to be bracing. And when she showed up at the briefing a little later, she was clean and refreshed.

Because the settlement was more like a small village than an encampment, most of the men had their families there, and those who did had their own houses. Thus, most of the meals were taken individually. But for those who were here without families, the meals were taken in the *comedor comunal,* or communal dining hall.

That was where the Code Name Team ate their meals and that was where, at 1900, just after a supper of beef and sweet potato stew, the men of the village began gathering for the briefing.

The Code Name Team had put the camp through a lot of training, not only the men who would do the fighting, but the women and children as well. Two bunkers had been built, and the noncombatants of the camp practiced running into the bunkers upon a signal to do so, the signal being the ringing of a steel hoop that hung from an arm just outside the headquarters building.

"Why do we need bunkers?" one man asked.

"Hopefully, we won't ever need them," John replied. "But if the time ever comes that we do need them, it will be nice to know that they're here."

In addition to the bunkers, John had the men build a berm from north to south, across the west end of the camp, and he put the men into positions behind the berms, having them establish fields of fire, and even discussed the concept of "final defensive fire."

Some of the men grumbled that they had joined the brigade to be a fighting force, not a defensive force, but the men who had their families in the camp with them were grateful for this added bit of security.

There had been several briefings over the last two weeks since the Code Name Team had arrived. That was because the team had conducted a rigorous training exercise for the Free Colombia Brigade and the meetings were after-action reports to discuss the lessons learned. Sometimes the meetings were just to disseminate routine information, or to discuss problems within the village.

But tonight would be different. The word was already out that this would be to discuss a real operation, and there was a degree of excited anticipation in the air. A few of the men exchanged teasing barbs, or machismo talk, such as what they, personally, would do to Mendoza if they caught him. But for the most part, the men were quiet and focused. They knew that if they went out on an actual operation, some of them would not return. The only question remaining was who that would be.

Ricardo Cortina stepped up to the front of the group, and when he did, the buzz of conversation stilled.

"My friends," he said. "Tonight, we shall strike a blow for our country."

The men cheered.

"Miguel?" Ricardo said, and the man who was third in command brought up an A-frame, upon which sat a white marking board covered by a cloth. As soon as he had the A-frame in place, he sat back down, and John stepped up to give the briefing.

John pulled the cloth back, revealing a detailed model of buildings, trees, etc.

"This is *Selva Acampa Uno*," John said, pointing to a group of buildings that sat in the middle of a lot of trees. "Jungle Camp One. Here, cocaine is produced for shipment and distribution all over the world, but primarily to the United States. It is not the largest camp in Mendoza's operation, but it was his first one, so if we destroy it, we will send a strong message that he is on notice."

"When do we do this, senor?" one of the men asked.

"Tonight," John replied, and his answer was met with loud cheers.

For the next several minutes, John laid out detailed plans as to how the operation would be conducted, from the approach, to the timing and order of battle, to the withdrawal. The men paid close attention to the instructions.

"Will you be in command, senor?"

"No," John replied. "My team and I will accompany you as advisers only. Ricardo is in overall command, but you will be divided into two teams. Esteban will lead Fire Team One, and Miguel Fire Team Two. Any questions on the operation?"

There were no questions.

"Those of you who have family here, take a few minutes to say your good-byes," John said. "Be back here in thirty minutes. Remember, carry nothing in your pocket that would identify you. If something happens, you don't want Mendoza's people to trace you back to your family."

"What about Manuel?" one of the men asked. "He is very famous for his tattoo. Everyone will know."

The others laughed.

"What is the tattoo?" John asked.

"It is nothing, senor. It is just a tarantula."

"That doesn't sound so bad," Linda said.

"Senorita, it is not the tarantula, it is where he has it tattooed."

Everyone laughed again, except for Manuel, who looked down in embarrassment.

"Oh my," Linda said. "If it's where I think it is, and there is enough room for a tarantula, you are *muchisimo un hombre!*"

Now everyone roared with laughter.

"Be back in a half hour," John called, dismissing the meeting.

After everyone left, the Code Name Team stayed behind, drinking coffee.

"Umm," Mike said, holding up his cup. "When a country can produce coffee like this, why the hell are they screwing around with drugs?"

"There's more money in drugs than there is in coffee," Chris replied. As Chris sipped his coffee, he was also busy cleaning his M-24 SWS, the sniper rifle he had purchased, along with the other weapons.

The M-24 was a .308-caliber, bolt-action rifle that would hold five rounds in its magazine. It had a barrel twenty-four inches long and a 10x24 Leupold Ultra M3A telescope sight.

"Are you going to be all right with that weapon?" John asked.

Chris picked it up and sighted down the barrel. "Yeah," he said. "This is a good piece."

Jennifer was also busy, putting several parcels into a large duffel bag.

"Okay, Paul, pick it up and see if you can carry it all right," she said.

Paul picked it up easily. "No problem."

"Good, then you'll be my bearer."

Paul laughed, then made a jungle sound, as if from a Tarzan picture. "Uhm gowa," he said. "Yes, Bwanna, me Paul, bearer and guide."

The others laughed as well.

"What do you have in there?" Linda asked.

"Oh, just a few fireworks," Jennifer replied.

"Oh, good. I like fireworks," Linda said.

"John, you want to come look at this?" Don Yee called. Don was sitting at a table with his laptop open in front of him.

"What have you got?" John asked.

"Here is the picture from the latest satellite pass," Don said.

"Can you print it out?"

"No problem," Don replied, punching the mouse. A moment later the portable printer began whirring, followed by a very detailed full-color print of the picture.

John studied it for a long moment. "When was this taken?"

"At 1732 hours," Don replied.

"There's something different here," John said.

"Looks the same to me," Don said.

"When was the previous picture taken?"

"About 1400."

"Have you got it?"

"Yes," Don said. He opened a folder and pulled out the picture, then handed it to John.

John studied it for a moment, then pointed to something. "At two o-clock there is nothing here." He picked up the latest printout. "But look at this one, taken at five thirty-two. Do you see this?" He put his finger on the picture. "What is this?"

"It looks like a bunker of some sort," Don said. "Let me call it back up on the screen."

Don struck a few keys and the picture came back up. He began enlarging it until the bunker was visible. "What is that?" he asked.

"Look, here and here," John said, pointing to each side of the bunker. "Wires?"

Don studied the picture a moment longer. "Yeah," he said. "It looks like it."

"Claymores," Jennifer said. Out of curiosity, she had come over to look at the picture as well. She pointed to lines that had attracted John's attention.

"These are arming wires," she said. "They transmit the signal to detonate the mines." She looked at the bunker for a moment. "Whoever is back here will be controlling them."

"Damn," Don said. "That wasn't here at two o'clock this afternoon. What made them decide to pick today to put them in?"

"Well, at least we now know they're there, thanks to you, Don," John said. "We'll just have to take care of them, that's all."

The others began returning then. Gone was the bravado and joking that had been in play earlier. Now all were serious, some were even frightened, though they exhibited a determination to go on, despite their fears.

There were a few women with the men, including Katy. She smiled at John.

"Are you surprised to see me?" she asked.

"Not entirely," John said. "I figured you didn't move out here for the food. If you are here, it's because you intend to be involved."

"I wish Brian had been as open-minded as you are," Katy said. She put her hand on John's hand, and he felt her fingers caressing his skin.

"We are all here, senor," Ricardo said.

"Ah yes, good," John replied. He walked over to stand beside Jennifer and the others from the Code Name Team. Jennifer put her hand on his, caressing his skin with her fingers.

"I wish Brian had been as open-minded as you are," she said quietly, mocking Katy.

"Hush," John said. "I can't help it if women are attracted to me."

Linda chuckled.

When all were gathered, Ricardo stood before them. He waited until they were silent. "*Vaya con Dios, mis guerreros valientes.*" Then to John and the others, he repeated it in English. "Go with God, my brave warriors," he said.

The men loaded into three pickup trucks. Then,

John led out in his HumVee, guiding the convoy with the GPS that was loaded with the geographic coordinates of Jungle Camp One. Mike was driving the second HumVee, bringing up the rear. The plan was to drive to within two miles of the camp, then hike in the rest of the way.

It was four o'clock in the morning when they reached a point that, according to the GPS, was exactly two miles from the factory. Here they stopped, then assembled as they were instructed.

"From this point on, no lights," John told them in their final briefing. "Those of you who are going with Esteban go this way." He pointed. "Those of you who are going with Miguel go this way. Esteban, you will hit them from the north. Miguel, you strike from the south."

"It would be better if my team strikes from the south," Esteban said.

"Why?"

"The team that strikes from the south has farther to go to get into position. I have more young men that Miguel."

"Ha, don't you worry about my *ancianos*," Miguel said. "We'll do just fine."

"Still, I think it would be better."

"All right," John said. Esteban, you strike from the south, Miguel, you from the north."

"Who will you be going with?" Miguel asked John.

"We'll form our own element and we'll strike from the west," John said, indicating the members of the Code Name Team. "That way we'll have them in a box. Remember, hit hard, hit fast."

John and the others of the team waited until both Esteban and Miguel were gone. "All right," he said. "Let's go."

"John, wait a moment," Chris said. He walked over

to the HumVee Paul had driven, then raised a panel on the floorboard in the back. He removed a canvas bag and took a pair of night goggles from it.

"Night goggles?" Mike said.

"Yeah. I didn't have enough for the others, so I thought it would be best just to keep them to ourselves."

"Good idea," John said, slipping on the goggles Chris handed him. The world around him suddenly grew much brighter, though it was in various shades of green.

The others donned the night-vision goggles as well.

"All right, let's go," John said. "We have to get there before the others do."

Jungle Camp One

The night-vision goggles facilitated their walk, allowing them to move through the woods at a ground-eating pace. In almost no time at all, they were at the edge of the camp. John used the small but powerful two-way radio.

"One?" he said. It was the only word he said.

"Yellow," Esteban replied.

"Two?"

"Yellow," Miguel answered.

The questions and responses were prearranged signals that let John know where they were. Both of them were within a mile, but more than half a mile, from the objective.

"All right," John said to his team. "Get ready, they'll be here soon."

"John, there's something strange here," Chris said. Chris had been examining the camp through light-gathering binoculars.

"What is it?"

Chris lowered the binoculars and shook his head. "I don't see anyone."

"Maybe they're all asleep," Mike suggested.

"Everyone? Even the guards? I don't think so."

"Well, this isn't the army," Paul said. "Maybe their guards just don't understand their duty."

"Yeah, well, I hope it's like that."

John's radio popped on. "One green," Esteban said, meaning that he was in position.

"Two green," Miguel said.

John looked at his team, saw that they were ready, then raised the little radio to his lips. "Move in," he ordered.

The two attack teams started moving toward the camp. Then, just as they reached the fence, scores of defenders, who had been hiding in ditches just inside the fence, rose up and began firing. Tracer rounds began streaming out of the camp from both sides, taking on Esteban's and Miguel's fire teams.

The two fire teams returned fire, but they were exposed, whereas the defenders had the cover of trenches. In addition, Claymore mines began going off. The Claymores were all facing Miguel's team and they were having a devastating effect.

"Chris, in the bunker!" Jennifer shouted. "That's the guy setting off the Claymores!"

Seeing the man Jennifer pointed out, Chris took aim and fired. The Claymore operator went down, stopping the heavy explosions, but doing nothing to lessen the amount of automatic weapons fire that was streaming out of the camp toward the two attacking elements.

"Senor! Senor! Miguel is dead!" a desperate voice cried over the radio. "Many are killed and wounded. What should we do?"

"Holy shit!" John said. "Esteban, Miguel, pull your men back! Pull your men back!"

Camp Bolivar

Back in the base camp, Don, who was set up in the dining room, called up a satellite picture of Jungle Camp One. He expected to see smoke and flames by now, and was surprised that the camp still appeared to be intact. Then he got an on-screen message from John.

> *Don*
> *They were expecting us. We were ambushed, losses are heavy.*

Don read the message, then looked over at Ricardo, who was talking to a couple of the wives of two of the men who were on the mission.

"Oh, I'm sure there is nothing for you to be nervous about," Ricardo said. "Our men are well trained and well armed. And God is on our side. So go home now and prepare a good meal for your husbands. They are heroes."

Reassured, the two women left the dining room. Ricardo glanced over at Don, who was sitting at his laptop, with a pained expression on his face.

"What is it, *mi amigo?* You look as if you have been bitten by a scorpion," Ricardo said.

"I think you should see this," Don said, turning the laptop around toward Ricardo.

Ricardo took his glasses from his pocket, then put them on carefully, hooking them over each ear. Using his finger, he slid the glasses up his nose, then leaned down to read the message.

After reading it, he looked back at Don with a pained expression on his face.

"What does that mean, they were expecting us?"

"It means we were set up," Don said.

"Set up?"

"Someone in our camp told them we were coming."

"But . . . how is that possible? Who could do such a thing?"

"I don't know," Don said. "You know these people, is there anyone among them that you aren't sure of?"

Ricardo shook his head defiantly. "No one," he said. "I would trust my life with anyone here."

"Well, I'm glad you feel that way, because that's exactly what you are doing," Don said. "You are putting your life, and the lives of others, in their hands. And one among them is betraying you."

Ricardo nodded, then left the dining room. Not until he was gone did Don tap back a message.

How many casualties?
Eight killed, including Miguel. Six wounded. We have recovered all the bodies and are bringing them home.

Neither Don nor Ricardo shared the message with the others in the camp, because they wanted to wait until all were back home. But they didn't have to share the information. Ricardo, who had been upbeat and encouraging earlier in the day, became morose as the day wore on. The others began feeding off of him. They didn't know if he knew anything they didn't know, or if he had just become a worrier, but whatever it was, it brought down the mood of the camp.

That might have had an ameliorating effect though, because when the attackers returned, carrying with them bodies and wounded, it was not as big a shock as it might have been.

Fortunately, only two of the dead were married, Miguel's and Esteban's second in command, Alvaro. The others gathered around the two widows to give them as much support as they could, though it was scant comfort to the women who had lost their husbands.

After the wounded were seen to, and arrangements were made for handling the dead, Ricardo asked for a meeting with Esteban, Palo, who had taken over for Miguel when he was killed, and the Code Name Team.

"What happened?" Ricardo asked.

"They were waiting for us," Esteban said.

"Waiting? How waiting?"

"They were hiding in long, deep ditches," Palo said. "As we approached, they jumped up and began shooting at us."

Ricardo pinched the bridge of his nose and shook his head. "This is my fault," he said. "I should never have sent them out like this."

"It isn't your fault, Ricardo," John insisted. "The men were well motivated, and you are the one who supplied the motivation."

"I motivated them to die," Ricardo said. "I wasted their lives."

"A lot of men have died for their country," John said. "These men are no different. They died with honor, and no one who dies with honor is wasted."

"Are we going to make another attack, Uncle?" Esteban asked.

Ricardo shook his head. "No," he said.

"Senor Cortina, you cannot give up now," Linda said. "If you did that, then their lives truly would be wasted."

"I need some time to think it over," Ricardo said.

"Uncle, while you are thinking about it, might I suggest that we promote Palo to take the place of Miguel?"

"Promote Palo? Yes, yes, of course," Ricardo said, almost absentmindedly. "Though that strikes me a little like rearranging the chairs on the deck of the *Titanic*."

Chapter 11

Luiz Mendoza was in the Round Table Room, enjoying a large slice of chocolate cake and a cup of Colombian coffee, when his cell phone rang.

"*Sí?*" he said.

"El Presidente, I have wonderful news to report," Gato said.

"What is it?"

"*Selva Acampa Uno* was attacked last night as we knew it would be. But the attack failed," Gato said.

Mendoza laughed. "So, our information was good."

"Yes."

"Tell me about it."

"It was raided during the night. But I am pleased to report that not one of our buildings was damaged."

"Our product?"

"Our product was not damaged, but three of our men were killed," Gato said.

"Send one thousand dollars to their next of kin," Mendoza said. "Who conducted the raid?

"It was just as our informant said. It was *Libere Brigada de Colombia.*"

"The Free Colombia Brigade," Mendoza spat, his words dripping with venom. "They are led by Ricardo Cortina, are they not?"

"*Sí*, Ricardo Cortina."

"I know him," Mendoza said. "He is the former judge who once sentenced me to die."

"I think you should know, El Presidente, that the Americans who are in our country, the ones who call themselves the Code Name Team, were on the same raid. They are working with *Libere Brigada de Colombia*."

"Offer a reward for the head of Ricardo Cortina. Five hundred thousand dollars, I will pay for his head, and I will pay an equal amount for the head of John Barrone."

"I will put out the word, El Presidente," Gato said.

Mendoza finished the conversation and folded his cell phone shut. He looked up just as Senator Josh Fitzgerald Kelly arrived. Smiling at the senator, Mendoza stood and extended his hand.

"Senator Kelly, it is so nice of you to come to New York to meet me," he said.

"Bushmills, eighty-nine, please," Senator Kelly said to the waiter who came to the table.

"You know your Irish whiskey, Senator," Mendoza said as the waiter hurried off to get his order.

"It's one of the finer things of my Irish heritage," Kelly replied. The senator was known to have a prodigious appetite for whiskey, and once, early in his senatorial career, while drinking, he drove his car off a bridge into a lake. An attractive young woman, Mannie Jean Katupa, was in the car with him. Senator Kelly managed to escape the sinking car, but Mannie, supposedly his secretary but believed by many to be his mistress, did not escape.

The two men sat at the table and Mendoza held up his coffee cup. "Pangean coffee," he said. "Like you, this is my heritage."

Kelly chuckled. "Pangean coffee? The world has learned to recognize, and appreciate, Colombian coffee. Are you really going to change the name and lose all that brand identification?"

"We'll get it back," Mendoza said. "By the way, I thought you might be interested in this." He handed Kelly an envelope, and the senior senator from Massachusetts opened it, then removed the letter.

> *Dear Mr. Mendoza*
>
> *New Power, the Political Action Committee that is dedicated to electing liberal-thinking men and women to the United States Senate, thanks you very much for your donation of one hundred thousand dollars.*
>
> *You may rest assured that we will be supporting candidates whose views are consistent with your own.*
> *Sincerely,*
> *Carl T. Simmons*

"Yes," Kelly said, handing the letter back to Mendoza. "You have chosen a good organization to work with."

The waiter returned with Kelly's whiskey and Kelly thanked him, then remained pointedly quiet, until the waiter left.

"I am told that New Power supports your campaigns," Mendoza said.

"They do," Kelly replied.

"Good, good, then we understand each other," Mendoza said.

"Do we, Mr. Mendoza?" Kelly asked.

"Of course we do," Mendoza answered. "I want Pangea to be a friend of the United States. And I want the United States to have a government of liberal-thinking, clear-headed senators and congressmen who are open-minded enough to recognize all the benefits of extending recognition to a new country."

Kelly took a swallow of his whiskey, then wiped the

back of his hand across his lips and stared across the table at Mendoza.

"You do know, don't you, that what you are asking for isn't going to be easy? There is a very, very strong element of opposition, not only to granting you official recognition, but to you ever becoming a country in the first place."

"Yes, I'm quite aware of that," Mendoza said. He flashed a disarming smile. "That's why I decided to start at the top."

"Well, hardly the top," Kelly said. "You'd have to go to the president for that."

"Hmmph," Mendoza said with a dismissive wave of his hand. "Your president has served but three years, and you have been in the Senate for how long? Thirty years?"

Kelly nodded. "Yes, thirty years."

"That's why I came to you. You will excuse me, Senator, but I come from a culture where the men on top don't last very long. So if you want to get something done, you first identify the problem, then you locate the person who can best deal with it. Senator Kelly, in this case, that would be you."

"I might be able to help you," Kelly said.

"I was hoping you might."

"But I feel I should tell you that one hundred thousand dollars is not nearly enough to garner that kind of support," Kelly added.

"I understand that. The one hundred thousand dollars has nothing to do with whatever arrangement we may come to. Let's call it a goodwill gesture. I am willing to pay handsomely if I can get what I want."

"What is handsomely? And what do you want?" Kelly asked.

"Five million dollars, perhaps more if our arrangement bears fruit. And if you wish, I will pay it directly to you."

Kelly held up his hand, palm out. "No, no, please, don't misunderstand me. I'm not talking about personal contributions, that would be bribery. And that would be wrong."

"Yes, of course."

"But many of my colleagues in both houses have tough political campaigns before them. Perhaps you could come up with some way to make certain that their campaigns are adequately financed."

"As I said, Senator, whatever you want, I will pay. And I'm not talking about bribery. I'm talking about legal campaign contributions."

"Good, good. That will give me something to work with," Kelly said. He tossed the rest of his drink down. "Now, what is that you want?"

"I want your government to recognize my country."

"I will do what I can," Kelly said. "But I can't guarantee that."

"I know. So, perhaps you can do something else for me."

"What would that be?"

"There is an armed band of guerrillas at large in my country. They call themselves the Free Colombia Brigade, but what they are is terrorists. In fact, they attacked one of my coffee plantations last night. Fortunately, the attack was beaten off, but three of my men, who were but simple coffee farmers, were killed."

"I'm sorry to hear that," Kelly said. "But I'm not sure what you want me to do. I can tell you without a doubt that you will not get American military aid to put them down."

"You misunderstand, Senator. I'm not looking for

American aid to come into the country. I'm wanting America to pull their aid out."

Kelly looked confused. "Now I don't understand what you are talking about," he said.

"There is an American paramilitary group operating in my country right now," Mendoza said. "They call themselves the Code Name Team, and they are sponsored by your CIA."

"I assure you, President Mendoza, I know nothing about them. Nothing."

"Then you should find out something about them," Mendoza said. "I mean, such organizations, working with the support of the CIA, but without the authorization of the Congress? Wouldn't that be illegal?"

"It is absolutely illegal," Kelly said. "And I assure you . . . I will get to the bottom of this."

"Thank you," Mendoza said. He smiled. "I'm sure we are going to have a very good working relationship."

Camp Bolivar

It had been one week since their operation against the drug factory, and since that time there had been several long discussions as to just what happened.

"Perhaps we should not have used the radio," Esteban suggested. "Maybe when we were using the radio they heard us."

"You didn't use the radio that much," Don said. "And when you did use it, it was in code."

"Maybe they interrupted the signals from the satellite," Ricardo said.

"No, even if they had, they wouldn't necessarily know they were about to be attacked. We have constant satellite surveillance of drug factories, all over the world," Chris said.

"I keep going back to the fact that they knew we were coming," John said. "They snatched Jennifer from the airport in Bogota, and they tried to kidnap . . . or kill Linda."

"Which brings us back to our original idea that we have a mole," John said.

"I just cannot believe that, senor," Ricardo said, shaking his head. "I cannot believe any in our camp would betray us."

"Wait a minute," Esteban said. "The weapons that your brought into camp. Where did you get them?"

"We got them from Viktor Marin," John said.

"Marin is the biggest *hijo de una puta* in all of Colombia," Esteban said. "If we have been betrayed, it was Marin who betrayed us."

"But how could he have learned of the details of our attack?" John asked. "We didn't even select the target until a couple of days earlier."

"It pains me to say this, nephew," Ricardo said. "But I fear that Senor Barrone is right. We must be very careful from now on."

"I agree," Esteban said.

After supper that night, John excused himself from the others and climbed the rope ladder to the top of one of the cliffs that bracketed the camp. Up here, out from under the canopy of the trees, he could see all the way to the coast, some three miles away. The stars were brilliant, and the full moon made a long, iridescent smear on the surface of the water. In addition, the white foam of the surf glowed brightly in the moonlight.

Though the colors of the flowers were dimmed by

darkness, their fragrance perfumed the night air,
while the evening breeze stirred the palms and rat-
tled the reeds. John was enjoying the scenery, and
the solitude, when he became aware that someone
else was up here, watching him. He hadn't seen or
heard anyone, but he knew he wasn't alone.

Slowly, and without being seen, John pulled the
Glock pistol from his holster. He slid the slide back,
chambering a round, then held the gun in front
of him.

"John?" It was the soft J sound, and he knew it was
Katy. What he didn't know was why she was up here.

"John?" she called again. "It's me, Katy."

Turning toward the sound, John saw her, but in silhouette only, as she was standing in the shadow of the
trees.

"Come on out," John called. "The view is beautiful
from here." Letting the hammer back down, he
checked to make sure the safety was on, then put his
pistol back in the holster.

"You are sure you don't mind?" Katy called from
the shadows.

"No, of course not. Why should I mind?"

"All right, then," Katy said, starting toward him.

John watched her emerge from the shadows,
watched until the silhouette took on shape, form,
and definition. Then, with a start, he realized that
Katy was naked!

Nude, and totally without embarrassment, Katy
closed the difference between them.

"Do you like?" she asked, stopping just in front of
him.

She was wearing a subtle perfume that was augmented by the understated note of her own musk.
She reached up to him, put her arms around his

neck, then leaned into him. He could feel the heat of her breasts, the insistent thrust of her pelvis.

"I thought you might like some company," she said, smiling up at him.

"Yes, company is nice," John replied. "I'm glad you came up. The view from up here is beautiful."

Gently, John took her arms down, then turned and walked away from her. "Come over here and look," he invited.

Katy was an exceptionally beautiful woman and had never been turned down by anyone before. As she stood there, watching him walk away, it took her a moment to realize that she had just been rejected.

John turned when he heard her walking away. He started to call after her, but checked himself. Nothing he could say would explain his action to her, so it was better just to leave it alone.

In fact, John wasn't that sure he could explain his action to himself. Why would he turn down an obvious offer of sex from a very beautiful woman? It wasn't out of loyalty to his wife, Michelle. She was dead.

It wasn't because of his relationship with either Jennifer or Linda. They were both working partners, and friends, but it had never progressed beyond that, nor would it ever. And he knew that Jennifer and Linda felt the same way. They would take a bullet for him . . . but neither of them was likely to go to bed with him, because if they did, it would change the whole dynamics of their relationship. And there was no way that the change would be for the better.

After allowing Katy enough time to return to the camp, John climbed back down himself. Jennifer was drinking a cup of coffee and sitting on a log close to a nearly extinguished campfire. As John approached she took a swallow of her coffee and studied him over the rim of the cup.

"I'm glad," she said.

"You're glad what?"

"That you didn't have sex with her."

"How do you know that I didn't? For that matter, how do you know that I even had the opportunity?"

"It's all over your face," Jennifer said.

John saw the coffeepot sitting on a grill over the fire. He picked up a cup and filled it.

"It's that obvious?"

"Not to everyone, perhaps," Jennifer said. "It is to me."

John chuckled. "Jeez, Jennifer, I'd hate to be married to you. I wouldn't be able to cheat."

"Ha, like you would cheat. You never cheated on Michelle, did you?"

"No. No, I didn't."

"Then you wouldn't cheat on me . . . or anyone. It's just not in your nature."

"I guess maybe you're right."

"That's why you didn't take Miss South America, or whatever beauty title she is, up on her offer. You would have been cheating on me."

"Oh?"

"And Linda, and Chris, Paul, Don, even Wagner. You would have been cheating on all of us."

John took a swallow of his coffee before he replied. Then he laughed, quietly. "Jennifer, you are as full of shit as a Christmas turkey," he said.

Chapter 12

Washington, D.C.

Senator Kelly was in Senator Harriet Clayton's office waiting on Ed "Tiny" Hallman. Tiny was Senator Harriet Clayton's new administrative assistant. Hallman had replaced her previous assistant, Henry Norton, when he got caught manipulating campaign finances.

Kelly and Clayton were often political allies, though in recent years both had higher ambitions than the U.S. Senate. Harriet had even started down the road toward seeking the nomination of her party, only to quit even as it was beginning to look like she might win. Since Harriet's loss of interest in the presidency, she and Kelly seemed to be getting along just a little better.

"Senator Kelly, how good to see you," Tiny Hallman said, stepping out of his office and extending his hand. Tiny, despite his name, or perhaps because of it, stood about six feet eight inches tall, and weighed in at 285 pounds. "What can I do for you?"

"Where is Harriet?"

Tiny looked at his watch, then chuckled. "She is involved in very important business," he said. "Right now she is getting her hair done."

"In the Senate shop?"

"Yes, sir. She should be back in about—"

"I can't wait," Kelly said. "I'll go find her."

"But, Senator—"

"Never mind, I know where it is," Kelly said, breezing out of the office before Tiny could stop him.

"Senator Clayton? Yes, you'll find her in the back, getting a rinse," a young, effeminate man said when Kelly went into the Senate beauty shop.

Kelly found Senator Harriet Clayton sitting in a chair, wearing a foil cap. She was reading a copy of *Time* magazine.

"Hello, Harriet," Kelly said.

"Josh," Harriet replied, surprised to see him. "What are you doing here?"

"A couple of years ago, when you had that little adventure in Sitarkistan . . . what was the name of the group that rescued you?"

"Why do you want to know?"

"Something has come up."

"What?"

"What was the name of the group, Harriet? You know I can find out somewhere else. You can just save me time, that's all."

"The name of the group was the Code Name Team. Now, what is this all about?"

"Are they sponsored by the government?"

"Sponsored by?" Harriet thought about the question for a moment. "No, I don't think they are sponsored by the government, but . . ."

"But what?"

"Well, when they rescued me, I had the distinct impression that, even though they weren't sponsored by the government, their activity was at least sanctioned."

"Damn, I'll bet that's it," Kelly said, snapping his

fingers. "Our cowboy administration is shooting from the hip again."

"Josh, why are you so interested in this?"

"Because I have it on very good authority that the Code Name Team is down in Colombia, right in the middle of this whole Pangea thing. If they are sponsored by our government, then we need to call the president to task on it. If they are acting on their own, then we need to let the world know that we have nothing to do with them, and we should stop them."

"Stop them? If they are in Colombia, how would you stop them?"

"By sending in a precision military strike force," Kelly said.

"Are you serious? You would send a military strike force into another country, to target Americans?"

"As far as I'm concerned, they aren't Americans, they are international terrorists."

"I don't know, I wouldn't be so quick to judge them, if I were you," Harriet said.

"I would expect you to think that. After all, they saved your life. But one good thing does not buy them the freedom to become mercenaries at large. Our, let us say, 'combative spirit' has caused the U.S. to suffer a loss of goodwill, prestige, and respect over the last five years. And outlaw gangs like this can only hurt us more."

"If you think having a bunch of independent mercenaries . . . who just happen to be Americans . . . is costing us friends in the international community, just what do you think would happen if we sent in the military? Colombia has not authorized military action against the FARC or the drug traffickers. What makes you think they would authorize this?"

"We wouldn't ask Colombia," Kelly said.

"You would send them in without getting permission? My God, Josh, have you gone daft? That would be an act of war."

"Oh, we would have permission all right, but not from Colombia. We would have permission from Pangea."

"There is no Pangea."

"There soon will be."

"Not as far as the U.S. Government is concerned," Harriet replied.

"Yes, well, I may be asking for your support on that, too. I'm going to propose that we recognize Pangea as soon as possible."

"Are you serious? That would be political suicide," Harriet gasped.

"Not if we played our cards right," Kelly said. "Especially, if you are dealt the right cards."

Something about Kelly's demeanor then caught Harriet's attention.

"What kind of cards are you talking about?" she asked, no longer the dissenter, but now an interested party.

"Suppose I told you that I had a very good meeting with Luiz Mendoza? And suppose I told you that, if the U.S. would grant recognition to his country, he would declare all drug trafficking to be illegal."

"Big deal, it's already illegal in Colombia, and look where that has gotten us."

"Yes, but in this case, Mendoza will conduct a very vigorous campaign to root out and destroy all the drugs grown in his country." Kelly smiled. "And who would be better able to do that than the son of a bitch who has been the kingpin behind all the drugs for the last several years? Think of it, Harriet. We have been fighting a national war on drugs ever since Reagan was in office. Have we been successful?"

"Not particularly," Harriet replied.

"'Not particularly' is a much more generous response than the program has earned," Kelly said. "The truth is, it hasn't been successful at all." Kelly's eyes started to sparkle. "But with Mendoza's help, which he will never offer except on a quid pro quo basis, we can finally make some progress against the war on drugs. In fact, Senator Harriet Clayton, I believe you and I could even hand the nation a victory in this battle."

"And you are willing to sacrifice the Code Name Team to achieve this?" Harriet asked.

"Sacrifices are sometimes made during war," Kelly said.

"Which you would know, because of your service in Vietnam," Harriet said. It was a gentle reminder that she was well aware of his actual service, as opposed to his public persona.

"What about it, Harriet? Do you want to be with me on this or not?"

"With you on what?"

"With me on exposing the way this president goes around Congress to get things done."

"By exposing the Code Name Team?" Harriet asked.

"Yes."

"Josh, have you considered the fact that exposing them could also put them in a great deal of danger?"

"Whatever danger they are in is of their own doing," Josh said.

Harriet shook her head. "Count me out on this one."

"What? Harriet, I can't believe this. You have always been a fighter for full disclosure. What has changed you?"

"I owe these people my life," Harriet said. "I will not be a party to putting them into danger."

"Well, you will excuse me if I don't have your same sense of loyalty to a group of mercenaries," Josh said.

Harriet watched Josh leave, then her stylist approach her.

"How are you doing, dear?" he asked, mincing, as he began peeling back some of the foil. "Oh yes, this is coming along quite nicely. I'd say about ten minutes more and you will be your own gorgeous self again."

Harriet started to go back to reading the magazine, but found that she could no longer concentrate. Instead, her mind went back to a time on the desert in Sitarkistan. She had been rescued from a terrorist cell by the Code Name Team, operating on their own, not with government support, though with tacit government approval. Then, just when they thought all was well, they learned they were about to be attacked by U.S. warplanes. One of the Code Name Team had managed to patch in to a defense communication satellite, and began desperately sending messages to the American warplanes.

Sitarkistan desert, two years earlier

"This is a message for U.S. warplanes in Sitarkistan on a strike mission for Bathshira," Don said. "Abort your attack. I say again, abort your attack. You are about to attack friendlies."

"Who is this?" asked a voice, obviously that of one of the pilots.

"I'm a friend," Don said. "Abort your attack."

"What is the recall authenticator?"

"I don't know," Don admitted.

"You don't know, buster, because there isn't one. Nice try, towel-head. Now, get off the air."

"No, I'm pleading with you. Do not attack. Do not attack. You will be attacking friendlies."

"I said, get off the air."

"U.S. Air Force pilot, this is John Barronne. I am the leader of a group of American mercenaries. We have rescued Senator Harriet Clayton. If you attack, you will be putting her in danger."

The air force pilot chuckled. "Mister, whoever you are, you are just giving me more incentive to attack."

"I told you who I am. My name is John Barrone."

"Well, Mr. John Barrone, if you are in the target area, I suggest you get your head down. I have strike orders and I intend to follow those orders."

"What are we going to do, John?" Chris asked.

"We're going to do what the man said," John said.

"What is it? What is happening?" Harriet asked. She had no earplug and therefore had been able to hear only one side of the conversation. "Is someone about to attack us?"

"I'm afraid so," John said. Looking toward the northwest, he saw them, four airplanes coming fast. "Here they are," he said. "Find some place to get down."

"What?" Harriet said. "This is ridiculous. I am a United States Senator! What is going on here?"

"Senator, you'd better get your ass down, or get it shot off," Jennifer said, sharply.

Little flashes of light appeared under the nose of each of the approaching planes. These were the Gatling guns and a second after the flashes began, the bullets began whizzing by, snapping through the trees and bouncing off the rocks around them.

"Take cover!" John shouted, leaping behind a rock formation.

Harriet didn't have to be told a second time. Screaming in panic, she also ducked behind some nearby rocks.

The airplanes roared overhead at that moment, each of them dropping something that tumbled through the air as they came down.

"Napalm!" John shouted.

The bombs hit all around the oasis, erupting into huge blossoms of fire. John could feel the searing heat of the blasts, but, fortunately neither he nor any of the others were directly in any of the blast areas.

The planes made a high, sharp turn, then came back. This time they were firing rockets and the rockets began exploding all around them. One of them hit the Land Rover, and it went up with a roar.

"Do something!" Harriet screamed. "Tell them to stop!"

"You heard me try, didn't you?" John asked.

"You didn't try hard enough," Harriet insisted.

"Well, if you think you can do any better, lady, you try," John said.

"John, wait!" Jennifer said. "That's it! Let her try!"

"What?"

"She's a famous person," Jennifer said. "A pain in the ass, but famous. Maybe the pilot will recognize her voice."

"Yeah," John said. "Yeah, that's a good idea." John took off his lavalier mike and handed it to Harriet. "Tell him to stop."

"How do I make it work?"

"I've set it to voice activation," John said. "Just speak."

Harriet nodded, then looked directly at the little microphone. "Listen to me, American pilot, whoever you are," she said. "This is Harriet Clayton, United States Senator from New Jersey. Harriet Clayton. You do know who I am, don't you?"

"I know who Senator Clayton is," the American pilot replied. "How do I know you are Clayton?"

"Listen to my voice, you Neanderthal military asshole!" Harriet said sharply. "Surely you have heard it before."

"Abort the attack," the voice said. "This is either Senator Clayton or someone who does a very good impression of the bitch."

"What? What did you call me? What is your name, mister? I demand to know your name!"

The four airplanes made a low pass over the oasis, flashing by in absolute silence for just a second, the silence then followed by the thunder of their engines. They wagged their wings as they pulled up and started away.

"Mr. Barrone?" the pilot's voice said.

"Yes."

"This is Colonel Joe M. Anderson. I apologize for the mixup. I'll have a rescue helicopter dispatched immediately."

"Thanks," John said.

Washington, D.C., today

Harriet smiled as she recalled that incident. It had been terrifying then, but now she took some pride in the fact that she had actually lived through it. Okay, so maybe the Code Name didn't treat her with the dignity she thought she deserved as a senator. She had come a long way since then. Then she was, as the young woman, Jennifer, had said, a pain in the ass. She had made a conscious effort to be less so now.

And she damn sure wasn't going to be a party to anything that put into danger the very men and women who had saved her.

Chapter 13

Code Name Safe House, Cali, Colombia

The house was on a long, hogback ridgeline, reached by only one road that wound its way up from the outskirts of Cali. Perched out on the very end of the hogback, the two-story, ten-bedroom house was cream-colored stucco, with a red clay-tile roof. A wide veranda extended along the side of the house, affording a very good view, not only of the city of Cali, but of the area just west of the city.

Esteban Cortina had located the house for the Code Name Team and it was to be their base of operations for the remainder of the time they would be in Colombia. He had just shown them through the house and now they were standing on the veranda. The house had been built right up to the very edge, so that from three sides, there was a sheer drop of almost two hundred feet to the ground below. It was not by accident that the house was chosen; its location was such that it could only be approached from one direction.

"I hope the house is to your satisfaction," he said.

Chris chuckled. "If we have to 'go to the mattresses,' this is a good place to do it," he said.

"I beg your pardon?" Esteban asked. "*Vaya a los colchones?*"

John laughed. "Chris is a big fan of the movie *The Godfather*," he said. *Vaya a los colchones,* go to the mattresses, means to hole up when things get hot."

Esteban looked confused for a moment, then he nodded and laughed. "*Sí, sí,*" he said. He made a sweeping wave of his hand. "This is a good place to go to the mattresses, *sí.*"

"You damn straight it is," Chris said. "I've never seen any place better."

"I will leave you here until we meet again," Esteban said.

"Esteban?" John called out as Esteban started to walk away.

"*Sí?*" Esteban stopped and turned back toward John.

"Who else knows that we are in this house?"

"Only Katy Correal knows," Esteban said.

"Why does she know?"

"She is the one who found the house."

"Yes, well, then we can't very well leave her out, can we? But tell no one else."

"Very well," he said. "I will tell no one."

John watched until Esteban got into his car and started back down the long, narrow, twisting road. Not until he was already in the car and on the move did John contact the rest of the team.

"Okay," he said. "Break up into pairs and go through this house. I want it swept from top to bottom. If you find anything, let me know."

"You got it, Chief," Paul said.

John went back into the kitchen where the refrigerator was already well stocked. He pulled out a beer and went into the den. One whole wall of the den was windows, overlooking the approach.

"I've got it," Don said.

"You've got what?" John asked.

Don was connecting some wires. "I've got the TV set to pull broadcasts down from the satellite. You want to see a little news from home?"

"Yeah," John said. "I'd like to know how my Red Sox are doing."

"Why?" Don asked. "They'll just break your heart again."

"Perhaps," John agreed. "But hope does spring eternal."

Don picked up the remote and pointed it toward the big screen. A picture came up. Stretching across the bottom of the picture was a long, orange line that ended with the NTS logo.

"Isn't that Senator Kelly?" Don asked.

"Yeah," John said.

"You had a run-in with him once, didn't you?"

John took a long swallow from his beer before he answered. "Yeah," he said, without elaboration.

"Senator, the president has stated publicly that the United States has no intention of recognizing Pangea, if, indeed, the country is formed. But you don't agree with him on that, do you?" The questioner was a young, very pretty blonde who was trying so hard to look intense that it was almost like a satire skit from *Saturday Night Live*.

"No, Emerald, I don't think it is a good idea to refuse to face reality. That is why I am calling for a hearing of the Senate Foreign Relations Committee to look in to granting President Designate Luiz Mendoza, and his newly formed government, immediate and full recognition."

"Would you tell us why?"

Senator Kelly was an old hand at TV appearances. In his years in the Senate, he had been on television many, many times. He looked directly into the camera and played to the audience at home.

"Look," he said. "During the twentieth century, the United States went from being a beacon of freedom for the whole world, to being the policeman of the world. And we weren't just an overbearing policeman, with our aggressive adventures in the Middle East, we have become the bad cop on the beat.

"I don't want to see us carry this same belligerent attitude into the twenty-first century. We have already made ourselves the holy enemy of the entire Muslim world. Now are we to tell a group of people who are peacefully creating a new nation that they cannot be free, that they cannot join the family of nations? Who are we to deny them their independence? And it is an independence won, I remind you, not by the barrel of a gun, but by the persuasiveness of diplomacy."

"But, Senator, there are those who say that this new nation of Pangea will be financed entirely by the illegal drug trade," Emerald said.

"Ah," Kelly replied, holding up his finger. "But illegal where?"

"Illegal here, in the United Sates," Emerald said.

"Precisely. The drugs are illegal here, in the United States," Kelly repeated. "Therefore, let us devote all our resources to combating drugs by stopping the trafficking, and by working hard to dry up the market. After all, Pangea could not sell drugs to us if we didn't have people here buying them. So you see, that is our problem, not the problem of the people of Pangea, who merely want freedom and independence."

"Thank you, Senator Kelly." The host turned toward the camera and smiled. "Our guest today has been Senator Josh Fitzgerald Kelly. Tune in tomorrow, when we will talk with weight-loss guru R.E. Spencer. This is Emerald Stacey. Good-bye for now."

A commercial popped up onto the screen.

"Royals beat the Red Sox," Don said.

"What?"

"Didn't you see the crawl across the bottom of the bottom of the screen? The Royals beat the Sox, four to three," Don said.

"Oh, uh, no, I didn't notice. But I'm sure you enjoyed telling me."

Don laughed. "Look, I'm going to go cook our dinner," he said, heading for the kitchen. "You want anything special?"

"No, whatever you fix is fine," John said.

After Don left, John turned off the TV and walked to the back of the house and stared through the window. One might think he was enjoying the view this particular advantage provided, but he wasn't. He was somewhere else now, somewhere long ago, and far away.

It happened several years ago, on March 12, 1986. On that day, Senator Kelly stood on the floor of the Senate, protesting the U.S. involvement with the ongoing revolution in Nicaragua.

The floor of the U.S. Senate, March, 1986

"I think this body should know that a plane that is supposedly carrying 'humanitarian aid' to the people of Nicaragua is in fact transporting weapons. This plane belongs to a Miami-based company, VivaAir, which is run by Larry Jensen, one of the largest marijuana traffickers in the United States. Despite Jensen's known history of drug smuggling, the CIA in general, and CIA agent John Barrone in particular, is working with Jensen in this illegal scheme."

John wasn't in Washington at the time, and had no idea that he had just been outed as a member of the CIA. In addition, Larry Jensen, who was an undercover agent for the DEA, had also been exposed.

That very night, agents for the Sandinistas found John's home in Alexandria. They waited, patiently, until John's wife, Michelle, returned from a shopping trip. As she was unloading groceries from her car, the Sandinistas pulled into the driveway behind her.

One of the Sandinistas got out of the car and began shooting at her with an AK-47. She went down with six bullet wounds, one of which severed her spine.

She lay all night in the driveway, discovered the next morning by the newspaper boy. John was called home and got to the hospital just before she died. He stood by her bed in the ICU ward, holding her hand, even though he knew she couldn't feel it, and didn't even know he was there. He stayed by her side until she died.

Code Name Safe House, Cali, Colombia, Today

"Is steak all right?" Don shouted. His shout brought John back to the present.

"What?" John replied.

"They've got a fantastic grill in here. I thought I'd cook us up some steaks."

"Yeah, sounds good," John said. He took out his billfold and opened it to the picture section. He stared at Michelle's picture for a moment, felt a lump come into his throat, then closed his billfold and put it away.

"All clean," Paul said, returning then, with the others. "We swept the entire house."

"Good," John said.

"Something smells good," Linda said.

John nodded toward the kitchen. "Don discovered the refrigerator," he said.

"What a surprise," Jennifer teased. "Don was the first one to discover the food. What are the odds?"

The others laughed.

"Where'd you get the beer?" Chris asked.

"In the refrigerator," John said. "We've not only got us a really nice house, it's well stocked."

"Yeah, it's amazing what kind of house you can rent for fifty thousand dollars a month, isn't it?" Mike said.

"Come and get it!" Don shouted. "Come and get it, or I'll throw it out."

"Ha! You mean come and get it, or you will eat it all," Chris said.

"Yeah, the day Don throws out food will be the day the sun rises in the west," Jennifer teased.

The Code Name Team stepped out onto the veranda where Don had set the table. He served them grilled steak and pork and beans, while Chris looked through the wine cart to come up with a good sauvignon for them.

For the next few minutes they did little but eat and rehash the operation they had just gone through.

"How the hell did they find out we were coming?" Chris asked.

"Obviously we have a mole. I mean, that's been evident from the very beginning," John said.

"How did they get the information out?" Mike asked.

"By satellite phone?" Linda answered.

"Yes, that would be my guess," John said. "But if whoever it is has access to a satellite phone, why didn't they tell them we would be hitting from both ends of the camp? If they had known that, they could have doubled the damage done by the Claymores. And we didn't make that decision until we were two miles from the camp, remember?" John said.

"Which means that whoever our mole is, he wasn't with our assault team," Paul said.

"Or she," Jennifer said.

"What?" Paul asked.

"You said 'he' wasn't with our assault team. What makes you think it's a he? It could be a she."

"Yes," John agreed. "You're right."

"Who's ready for some ice cream?" Don said.

Over ice cream, they began discussing their next operation.

"We're going to be handling this next operation by ourselves," John said.

"No help from the Free Colombia Brigade?" Chris asked.

"No. I think it's best we keep this one as quiet as we can. It is absolutely essential that we get in and out, without our plans being compromised. Whoever the mole is, I don't want to give him . . ." He paused, looked at Jennifer, and smiled. "Or her," he amended, "a chance to screw this one up."

"I agree," Jennifer said.

"I want this to be a clean, surgical hit. To be honest, even if I didn't suspect a mole within the battalion, I would want us to do this one by ourselves."

"Is it another factory?" Paul asked.

"No, not a factory," John said.

"What is it, then? One of Mendoza's army units?"

John laughed. "No, when we hit an army unit, we will be using Cortina and his group. Our target for this operation will be the compound of one of the leading drug kingpins in the whole country. And if our information is right, there will be several million dollars in cash on the premises."

"Ha!" Paul said. "No wonder we don't want anyone else to know."

"Then our target is the money," Jennifer said.

"No, the money is our goal," John replied. "Our Target is Gilberto Escobar."

"Escobar? Wait, wasn't there a Pablo Escobar killed in 1993?" Linda asked.

John nodded. "You know your Colombian drug history, I see. Yes, there was a man named Pablo Escobar who was killed in a shootout with the Colombian Army. Pablo Escobar was known as the king of the Medellin Cartel."

"So, is this . . . Gilberto Escobar related to Pablo Escobar?"

"Nobody really knows," John said. "He may be related, or he may have just taken the name for whatever business advantage he believes it offers him. But whether he is related by blood or not, he is certainly related by his activities. Escobar is one of the leading drug lords in the country right now, just one tier down from Mendoza himself."

"Are he and Mendoza rivals?" Paul asked.

"They have been in the past," John said. "And they would have been again in the future, but for now they are allies in this scheme to break away from Colombia and become Pangea."

"You said Escobar would have been Mendoza's rival

in the future," Jennifer said. "That's an odd way of putting it. What do you mean by would have been?"

"Oh," John replied easily, as he ate the last spoonful of his ice cream, "I mean he would have been if he lived long enough. But Escobar isn't going to be around long enough to be Mendoza's rival, because I plan to kill the son of a bitch."

Chapter 14

Escobar Compound in remote southeast Colombia

The centerpiece of the Gilberto Escobar compound was a huge, two-story white house. The top floor was completely surrounded by a balcony, the bottom floor by a veranda, and on all four sides of the house the balcony and veranda were patrolled by guards.

Surrounding the house was a large, closely trimmed lawn, maintained not so much for its appearance, though it was attractive, as for its security. With the open lawn the house could not be approached without the intruder being seen.

Two HumVees and a Mercedes stretch limousine were parked in the curved driveway. To the north of the house was an impressive array of antennae and satellite dishes, providing Escobar with an electronic link to the rest of the world.

The east lawn was the longest. Whereas the other three sides of the house had no more than fifty yards of open ground, on this side there was a run of at least a hundred yards between the house and the adjacent jungle. And it was on this side of the house, just at the jungle's edge, that John Barrone and the others of the Code Name Team had taken up positions.

Halfway between the Code Name Team and the house was a helipad, upon which sat a Hughes 500 helicopter, the same model used by the military and designated the OH-6.

It was still dark, though a faint lightening of the sky could be seen behind them. The four men and two women were dressed in jungle fatigues, and their faces were blackened with dark green camouflage paint. Only Don Yee had been left behind, but John was in communication with him through a direct-link text-message exchange. He received his first message, then tapped in a reply.

DON: Are you in position?
JOHN: Yes.
DON: It is 27 minutes until dawn, 32 minutes until satellite is in position for first look.
JOHN: We will stay put until then.

John looked over toward Jennifer, who was next to him. He pointed to his watch, then flashed his full hand six times, then held up two, indicating that they had a thirty-two-minute wait. Jennifer nodded, then relayed the message on to Chris, who sent it forward until, within a few seconds, the entire team had been notified.

John could hear the mosquitoes buzzing all around him, but he resisted the impulse to slap at them, depending instead upon the mosquito repellent he had applied before they left.

The morning birds began to chirp and sing, while the high, keening sounds of the night creatures fell silent.

It grew lighter.

"Miguel," one of the guards shouted. "*Tengo que hacer pis!*"

"*Usted puede esperar media hora.*"

"No, I can't wait half an hour," he said in English. "I have to piss now."

John saw the guard walk over to the edge of the porch. He stood there for a moment, then began peeing, the arc glistening once in the first shaft of morning sun.

John got another message from Don.

DON:	Get ready for satellite pass. You want visual or infrared?
JOHN:	Let's have both.
DON:	Okay, here comes visual.

John studied the screen. He saw the house from above, giving him a visual picture of the entire surroundings, including outbuildings and structures on the other side of the house that he could not see from where he was lying in wait.

John captured the picture, then saved it in case he needed it later.

The next picture to come up was very similar to the first, except this one was infrared images. It showed the whole screen in shadow, but with bright blips anywhere there was more heat than the surrounding area. The first thing he noticed was the tree line where he and the other Code Name Team members were waiting. He could see, quite clearly, six bright blips, representing the six of them. He could also see the guards around the house. What he was especially interested in determining was whether or not there were any roaming patrols around the house. There didn't seem to be any.

John signaled for the others to gather around him. When all were present, he showed them the two pictures, first the visual, then the infrared.

"All right, look," John said. "You see these guards,

the ones on the north and south side of the house?
They are going in the same direction so that both
of them are down at the far end, that is, the west end
at the same time. I've been watching them. It takes
them thirty seconds to come back down to this end."

"What about the north and south guards on the
bottom porch?" Chris asked.

"Well, that might be a problem," John admitted.
"They are sort of coordinated with the two on top,
but not quite. When the top two are at the far end,
these two are a quarter of the way back already. But
you see these bushes at this end of the porch? If we
are halfway across the lawn by the time those two
start back, the bushes should block their view of us."

"So, we have to cover fifty yards in about ten seconds," Jennifer said.

"Yeah but, come on, how hard can that be?" John
asked. "There isn't a high school runner in the country who can't do one hundred yards in ten seconds."

"There isn't a high school runner in the country
who is forty years old, trying to keep from being
seen, and carrying forty pounds of gear," Paul said.

"Ahh, it's a piece of cake," Linda said. "Think back
to your football days. This can't be harder than running through a couple of Michigan linebackers."

"I was young, strong, and stupid then," Paul said.

"Well, so you're no longer young and strong," Linda
said. "You can still do it, I've got confidence in you."

It took the others a second to catch Linda's omis-
sion and when they did, they laughed. The laugh was
a needed break from the tension.

John pointed to the blips on the balcony. "Chris,
I need you to take these guards out. Both of them,"
John said, pointing to the two blips on the east side
of the house. One of the blips was on the upstairs
balcony, the other on the downstairs porch.

"All right," Chris agreed.

"As soon as the guards are down, we start running, balls to the wall, for the house. Jennifer?"

"Yes," Jennifer replied.

"Get to the helicopter and blow it up."

"Oh, wow, that's a million dollars," Linda said.

"You think you can fly it out of here?" John asked.

Linda shook her head. "No. Don's been teaching me, but I'm not confident enough yet to try to fly it."

"Then we don't have any choice. We have to destroy it," John said. "Linda, when we start toward the house, you go with Jennifer. Provide her with cover while she rigs the explosives. After you get the chopper rigged, take care of the vehicles in the driveway."

"What about us?" Paul asked. "What do we do once we reach the house?"

"Paul, you will come with me. Chris, you are going to stay here."

"What, and miss the fun?" Chris complained.

"Sorry 'bout that, but I need your shooting eye," John said. "You stay ready, and if you see anyone threatening us, shoot the son of a bitch."

"You got it," Chris replied.

"All right, everyone, get ready."

Chris wrapped the sling around his arm, raised his rifle, and waited. John watched until the other two guards were at the far end of their route.

"Now," he said.

Phfttt!

The sound of the shot was so subdued that none of the guards heard it. Even as the guard on the balcony went down, Chris was operating the bolt, slamming another cartridge into the chamber. He aimed a second time.

Phftt!

"Okay, let's go, John said.

John, Paul, Jennifer, and Linda started across the open lawn, running in a crouch. Jennifer and Linda stopped at the helicopter, John and Paul continued on to the house.

John pointed to the other end of the porch, then made a cutting sign across his neck. Paul nodded back, then pulled out a small, claw-shaped knife called a karambit. He waited in the bushes and when the guard reached the end of the porch right above him, he reached up and jerked him down.

"*Qué—*" the guard started, but that was as far as he got before Paul slashed his hand across his throat.

John's guard had not made it to the end of the porch yet, so John was able to climb over the banister, then step behind the corner and wait. When the guard reached the end of the porch, he looked over and saw the two bodies, the one Chris had killed and the one Paul had killed.

Gasping, the guard started toward them. As he did so, John stepped out from the corner and took him down with a smash to the end of his nose. That blow sent bone fragments into his brain, killing him instantly.

"Paul," John said quietly.

"Here."

Paul stepped out of the bushes and joined John in the middle of the porch. John tried the door, but it was locked. Paul shoved his elbow through the glass right beside the door handle, then stuck his hand in through the hole he had just made and unlocked the door from inside.

"Damn," Paul said as they stepped into the room. "The son of a bitch lives well, doesn't he?"

The floor of the room was white marble. The furniture was expensive, as was the statuary, though the statuary was rather gaudy.

"Whoa, look at that," John said quietly, nodding toward the fireplace. Over the mantel was a huge painting, on black velvet, of a bullfighter.

"You have to really admire this guy's taste, don't you?" Paul said sarcastically.

The two started up the stairs. At the top a door opened and a young woman stepped out into the hall. She was young, beautiful, and absolutely naked.

Her eyes grew very large when she saw Paul and John, and she took in a breath as if to scream, but John pointed his pistol at her and shook his head no. He put his finger over his lips, cautioning her to be quiet.

The young woman didn't make a sound.

"Do you speak English?" John asked.

The young woman shook her head, but said nothing.

"The door to Escobar's bedroom," John said. "Which one is it?"

Silently, the woman pointed to a door.

"Go downstairs and stay out of the way, if you don't want to get hurt," John said.

The young woman nodded, then moved quickly to the stairs and hurried down.

At that moment one of the guards on the balcony happened to pass by a window and, glancing in, saw John and Paul standing in the hallway, holding pistols.

"*Intrusos! Tenemos a intrusos!*" the guard shouted loudly.

At almost the same time the guard gave the alarm, he opened fire with his AK-47, shooting through the window. The bullets sprayed the wall between John and Paul, hitting a vase that was sitting on a stand in the hallway.

The vase shattered as John and Paul dived to the floor. John shot back, killing the guard who had shot at them, while Paul rolled over once, then came up in position to shoot the other guard who, upon hearing the shooting, had hurried up to see what it was.

"*Alarma, alarma! Intrusos!*" a voice shouted from another part of the house.

Within seconds three more men were racing up the stairs, spraying automatic weapons fire indiscriminately. John and Paul could hear the bullets whizzing by as they slammed into the walls behind them. They returned fire and the three went down.

There was someone else at the far end of the hall, a tall, dark, bearded man. With John's and Paul's attention diverted by the men on the stairs and the others below, they were unaware that they were being targeted by the bearded man.

There was the tinkling sound of something popping through a glass window. Before the bearded man could pull the trigger a bullet crashed into his temple, killing him instantly.

It wasn't until then that John noticed him.

"I see Chris is on the job," Paul said.

"Yeah," John agreed. "We've got to get into Escobar's bedroom."

"Go for it," Paul said. "I'll cover you."

"Why don't you go for it and I'll cover you?" John said. "You were the football player. It should be easy for you."

"Yeah, but you're the chief," Paul said. "The honor is all yours."

John waited for a moment, then he sighed. "All right," he said. Taking a deep breath, he got up and ran toward the door leading into Escobar's bedroom. "Oh, shiiiiit!" he yelled as he ran.

He kicked the door open in midrun, then burst into the room, falling to the floor and rolling to the right with his gun extended and ready.

The bed was empty, except for two naked women who sat in the middle, clutching each other in fear.

"*Donde esta el?*" he shouted.

The women pointed toward the hanging draperies. John moved toward the end of the drapes, all the while keeping his gun extended and ready. He pulled on the cord, was pleasantly surprised to see that it was a power cord, and the drapes opened automatically.

He dropped to one knee and waited for the drapes to open, expecting to see Escobar hiding behind them.

Escobar wasn't there.

The window was open.

Stepping up to the open window, John saw someone running toward the helicopter. He fired at him but it was a difficult shot with a pistol and he missed.

"Shit!" he shouted.

At that moment Paul came into the room just behind him.

"Where is he?" Paul asked.

"There," John said, pointing to the helicopter pad.

Like John, Paul took a shot. And like John, he missed.

"Did you see anybody else?" John asked.

"No," Paul answered. "It just got real quiet all of a sudden."

They heard the ascending hum of a turbine engine being started. Then, as the blades began spinning rapidly, the helicopter lifted up from the pad. While it was still hovering on its ground cushion, Escobar turned the helicopter toward the house. As he did, something dropped down from just under the nose.

"What the hell? He has a minigun on that thing!" John shouted.

Escobar opened fire. The gun, with an effective rate of fire of four thousand rounds per minute, smashed through the window and scattered rounds all over the room. John and Paul dived for the floor, saved only by the fact that there was a twenty-four-inch marble base all the way around the floor.

The two women on the bed weren't as lucky, and when John glanced toward their bloody bodies, he saw that both were dead, hit many times.

The firing stopped and John crawled back over to the window, then raised himself up to have a peek. He saw the helicopter turn away, then the nose dip down as it started racing across the open ground. It began to climb and John cursed himself for missing him.

Suddenly there was a bright flash of light, followed by a large red fireball and a puff of smoke. A second later the sound of the explosion reached them, a low, flat, stomach-shaking *kerwhump*.

Pieces of the helicopter rained down onto the lawn.

"Damn," Paul said. "Jennifer does know her business, doesn't she?"

"We'd better see who's left," John said.

Cautiously, the two men began searching the rest of the house.

Outside the house, Chris had come up to join Jennifer and Linda and the three of them watched the helicopter lift up, then fire into the house.

"Damn!" Jennifer said. "I should've put a remote rather than a timer on that bomb."

They watched the helicopter spray the house, then turn and start its takeoff run. It reached about a hundred feet when the bomb went off.

"All right!" Jennifer said. "Now, let's—"

"Jennifer!" Linda shouted and she pointed to two men who were running toward the cars. When the men saw Chris and the two women, they started shooting.

Chris, Linda, and Jennifer returned fire. Both of the men went down, then, for a long moment, there was nothing but quiet. Even the birds had quit singing, frightened into silence by the gunfire.

John and Paul came out onto the upstairs balcony.

"Everyone all right down there?" John called.

"Yeah," Jennifer replied. "What about you?"

"We're okay."

"Anyone left?"

"I don't think so," John said. "But come on in and have a look around. Be careful."

Jennifer and the others went inside and were met by John and Paul, who had come back down the stairs. Three women were in front of John and Paul, all three naked and terrified.

"Linda, you want to take charge of the women?" John asked. "I've told them they have nothing to fear from us, but I'm not sure they believe me."

"You!" Chris suddenly shouted. "Come out of there! *Venga aquí!*"

Chris was shouting toward a door at the back of the room, and he and the others pointed their guns in that direction.

"*Por favor, no disparar. Somos solo criados!*"

"You are servants, huh? Well, come on out. We won't shoot," John said.

Three men came out with their hands up. One of them was dressed as a butler, one as a chauffer, and the third was in cook's whites. They looked around in awe and fear at the carnage. All three crossed themselves.

"*La piedad de Dios estar con usted,*" the man in the butler's outfit said.

"God's mercy be with them, huh?" John said.

"Well, God can have mercy on them, I sure don't. What's your name?"

"*Mi nombre es Fidel.*"

"Well, Fidel, do you know where the safe is?"

Fidel and the others looked at him.

"You do speak English, don't you, Fidel?"

"*Sí.* Yes."

"Where is the safe? Where did Escobar keep his money?"

"*No digales!*" one of the naked women shouted.

John looked back toward her. "Don't tell us, huh? So, that means you do know where the safe is?"

The naked woman glared at John. "I don't know," she said. "None of us know. It was a secret kept from us."

"And you are?"

"Maria."

"Well, Maria, why did you shout at Fidel not to tell? If he doesn't know, he couldn't tell me, now, could he?"

Paul had been watching the servants, and he saw Fidel glance quickly toward the fireplace mantel.

Paul laughed. "I'll be damned," he said.

"What is it?" John asked.

"Turns out Escobar's originality was about as well developed as his taste."

"What do you mean?" Jennifer asked.

"Fidel just told me where the safe is," Paul said.

"Fidel!" Maria hissed, angrily.

"I said nothing," Fidel protested.

"Don't get mad at Fidel. He didn't know he told me," Paul said.

Paul walked over to the fireplace, then reached up and took down the big, oversized painting-on-velvet of the bullfighter. Behind the painting was the door of a safe.

"Ha!" John said. "No wonder he had that painting there. The son of a bitch probably couldn't find another one big enough. Jennifer, do you think you can get it open?"

"I'm sure I can. Just give me a few minutes," Jennifer said. "But you'd better get everyone out of here."

Linda spoke to Maria and the other naked women while Chris took charge of Fidel and the servants. They moved them all out onto the front porch. Paul came out with them, while John stayed inside and watched as Jennifer placed the claylike C-4 around the hinges of the safe. She worked quickly and deftly, then connected a blasting cord and started backing away. Glancing over her shoulder, she saw a big sofa.

"We had better get down behind that," she said.

The two squatted behind the sofa, then Jennifer squeezed the generator.

The C-4 exploded with a loud thump, and the door was blown off the safe. They could hear it flying by as it passed over the sofa, tumbled a couple of times, then landed with a clang on the marble floor where it rocked back and forth for a few seconds. Not until all was quiet did John and Jennifer rise up and glance through the little cloud of white smoke, toward the safe.

"Good job, Jennifer," John said, smiling. "It blew cleanly."

The two went over to look at the safe. It was as large as a footlocker, and it was filled to the top with bound bills. John whistled softly. "All U.S. dollars," he said. "Not one peso."

"How much do you think is here?"

John picked up one packet. It was in one-hundred-dollar bills. Most of the packets were the same, though here and there were a few fifties and twenties.

"I couldn't guess," John said. "But I'd say there's enough here to buy us all a good dinner tonight."

Jennifer laughed.

John walked back out onto the porch where Paul, Chris, and Linda were keeping an eye on their nine prisoners, who were sitting down against the porch railing.

"Fidel," John said, "do you think you could come up with any sacks or bags we could use?"

"Perhaps there are some bags in the kitchen," Fidel said.

"*No tengo ningunos sacos que son vacíos, Fidel,*" the cook replied.

"He says he has no empty sacks, senor," Fidel translated.

"Then tell him to empty some and bring them into the great room."

"*Sí,* I will do so," the cook replied, indicating by his response that he could speak English.

"Paul, go with him to keep an eye on him," John ordered. "The rest of you, come with me."

A moment later Paul and the cook returned with several large burlap bags.

"Start filling them with money," John ordered, and Fidel, Maria, the cook, and the others began working. It took about five minutes before they were finished. Then John reached down into one of the bags and pulled out nine packets of one-hundred-dollar bills. He tossed a packet to each of the servants and to the naked women.

"Here," he said. "Buy yourselves something to wear."

At first they were confused, then Fidel put it into words.

"Senor, this money, it is for us?" he asked.

"Not enough?" John asked. He pulled out nine

more packets and distributed them. "Okay, there you go. But don't ask for any more."

As they realized now that, not only were they not going to be killed, but they were being rewarded, huge smiles broke out on the faces of all of them.

"*Gracias, senor. Muchas gracias!*" Fidel said.

"You're welcome."

"John, what about the cars?" Jennifer asked. "The ones in the driveway."

"What about them?"

"I didn't get the charges laid."

"Let them have them," John said, taking in the others with a wave of his hand.

"Senor, one moment, please," Fidel said, holding up his hand.

John stopped and watched as Fidel walked over to a cabinet. He opened the doors and took out four bottles of champagne.

"Dom Perignon, 1959," he said. "Enjoy."

"Why, thank you, Fidel," John said. "I hope there is some left for you folks to enjoy."

"Don't worry, senor, there is enough."

John waved good-bye, then he and his team hurried back across the open lawn and into the jungle, where they would have a two-mile trek back to their vehicles.

"John, did he say this was vintage 1959?" Jennifer asked.

"Yes."

"That stuff is over five hundred dollars per bottle. You sure you want to drink that?"

"Drink it, as opposed to what?" John asked.

Jennifer laughed. "You have a point there," she said.

"You think those girls are dressed yet?" Chris asked.

"You worrying about them, are you?" Linda teased.

"Well, you know, they could catch cold or something."

Paul chuckled. "Right, in eighty-five-degree weather."

"Well, it has to be embarrassing, being naked in front of the others."

"I wouldn't worry about it, Chris," John said. "My guess is that, by now, they aren't the only ones naked."

Chapter 15

Harley Thomas sat in his living room, watching the news. After several stories concerning the Mideast, the focus switched to Colombia. The picture was of a large, beautiful house in a lush, tropical setting. There were several policemen and vehicles on the scene.

"Police made a grizzly discovery here at the palatial estate of Gilberto Escobar, located some twenty miles southwest of Popayan," the reporter was saying.

"Here, police found no fewer than twelve bodies on the premises. Another body was found in the wreckage of a helicopter.

"Police are theorizing that the violence was related to a drug war between rival gangs, but they are surprised by that, because Escobar and Mendoza had recently formed an alliance to bring about the secession of Pangea. Pangea is the proposed name for the new country that Mendoza would create, by carving away a large section of Colombia."

The phone rang and because it was right beside the sofa, Harley picked it up.

"Thomas," he said.

"It's me." Harley recognized the voice of his next higher, the deputy director. "You saw the news?"

"I'm watching it."

"Are we culpable?"

"No."

"You are sure you people didn't do this?"

"That's not what you asked," Harley said. "You asked if we are culpable, and I said no."

"Senator Kelly is going to call for a congressional inquiry into the situation in Colombia."

"There should be an inquiry."

"My point is, Harley, if you have to, can you call them back in?"

"Can I call who back in?"

The deputy director sighed. "You're right. Forget that I called."

"What call?" Harley asked.

There was a click on the phone as the deputy director hung up.

"Who was that, dear?" Harley's wife called from the kitchen.

"Wrong number," Harley replied.

"Ah yes," she said. She had been married to him long enough to realize that "wrong numbers" did not always mean wrong numbers. And she had been married to him long enough to understand that it was best not to pursue the subject any further.

"Dinner's ready."

"Umm," Harley said, getting up from the sofa. "It smells good."

Article in the American News Daily

By Michael Lindell,
Special to the *American News Daily*

POPAYAN, COLOMBIA—After Luiz Alberto Mendoza demanded in early June that all mayors in the section of the country he designates as Pangea leave town, more than 200 municipal executives quit in fear. He called for such a move because it is his intention to appoint new mayors once the new country is established.

Several recent standoffs between indigenous towns and armed Pangea activists have led some of Colombia's elite to embrace civil resistance as a way to express their own disapproval of the upcoming secession. Ricardo Cortina, former senator and judge, is leading a group called the Free Colombia Brigade, which is fighting again secession.

Mr. Cortina came into prominence a few months ago, when he led protests against the Pangean Revolutionary Group in the towns of Totoro and Toribio. Here, in the southwestern province of Cauca, the largely indigenous communities marched in the streets to defend their elected officials when the Pangean Revolutionary Group arrived.

The PRG retaliated by launching a 72-hour siege of both towns, gravely wounding many civilians. In Toribio, they held 14 policemen hostage, threatening to burn them alive. But the townspeople, helped by the local priest, implored the PRG to respect the lives of the policemen, and they were ultimately let go. The local PRG commander told a television station that they did not kill the officers because they acted like "true men."

"What does the PRG really want?" Cortina asks. "A free and independent country? No. What they want is a means of perpetuating the scourge of drug production and exportation. They are an organization without values, or principles. That is why we have formed the

Libere Brigada de Colombia" (Free Colombia Brigade).

Uriz doesn't have high hopes for help from the Colombian administration, which he believes has sold out a great portion of the country.

Washington, D.C.

Unable to convince the Senate Foreign Relations Committee to convene a hearing on the situation in Colombia, Senator Josh Fitzgerald Kelly assembled a subcommittee hearing, made up only of members of his party. Because it was not a full committee, their findings would have no weight, but Senator Kelly was often mentioned as a potential candidate for president of the United States and much of the press, especially the liberal press, gave his committee all the exposure and weight of a full committee.

Kelly was somewhat disgruntled by the fact that he was not allowed to use the meeting room normally used by the Foreign Relations Committee.

"If we allowed you to use the room, it would give the appearance of an official inquiry into the matter," the chairman of the committee told him.

"Fine," Kelly said sarcastically. "Just where do you propose that I hold these hearings?"

"They aren't hearings," the chairman said, quickly holding up his finger to interrupt Kelly. "They are meetings."

"All right, meetings. Where do you propose I hold them? In the parking lot?" he asked sarcastically.

"Oh, I hardly think you would have to go to that extreme," the chairman said. "In fact, I have made arrangements with the chairman of the Senate Committee on Indian Affairs. He has agreed to let you use their meeting room in the Russell Building. It is room 485."

"The Committee on Indian Affairs," Kelly said with a scoff. "Nothing important has been discussed in there since George Armstrong Custer."

"Well then, perhaps your group can bring some luster to it," the chairman suggested.

Russell Senate Office Building, room 485

The meeting room was considerably smaller than the one for the Foreign Affairs Committee, thus accommodating far fewer people than Kelly would have wanted. It was dominated by the bronze statue of an Indian, on one knee, pointing his arched bow upward, his arm and hands in the position of drawing it back to release an arrow.

"Can I move this?" Kelly asked the chairman of the Indian Affairs Committee.

"Absolutely not," the chairman replied. "That was done by the great Indian sculptor Alan Houser. It is called *Rain Arrow*, and we are very proud of it."

"All right, I was just asking, that's all." Kelly checked his watch. He had about twenty minutes until the meeting started. He knew that some of the press corps had already arrived, but they wouldn't be allowed into the room before five minutes till. His cell phone rang.

"Yes?" he said, flipping it open.

"I just thought I would give you an update, Senator," his AA said. "Mendoza is on his way to attend the meeting."

Kelly smiled broadly. "Good, then he did accept my invitation. Thanks, Tim."

Kelly snapped the phone shut and put it away. Mendoza's presence would absolutely guarantee press coverage. The only question was, would Mendoza get top billing?

Damn, Kelly thought. *I should have thought of that.*

Half an hour later, with four other members of the Senate Foreign Relations Committee from his own party present, Kelly brought the gavel down sharply, calling the room to quiet.

"I hereby call to order . . ." Kelly started to say meeting, then got a better idea. "This Foreign Relations Caucus on conditions in Colombia."

Kelly checked the faces of the newspeople and could tell from their reactions . . . some were even nodding in agreement . . . that his choice of words had played well with them.

"The purpose of this caucus is to examine the situation in Colombia. Should, or should not, the United States grant recognition to the nation of Pangea? That is the question we will be asking, and I am instructed to inform you that the answer we come up with is not to be construed as an official declaration by the Senate Foreign Relations Committee. However, we will make our findings known to the committee, and I will read our findings into the congressional record. I now call our first witness."

Chapter 16

CIA Headquarters, Langley, Virginia

Headquarters for the Central Intelligence Agency is in Langley, Virginia, across the Potomac and seven miles north of Washington. A flashing red light cautions anyone who might inadvertently turn onto the approach road. Should they continue, they will come to a guardhouse that is manned twenty-four hours per day. Here, unless they are authorized, they will be turned back. There are no public tours, no facilities for visiting.

Those who are authorized will be given a badge that is color-coded to grant them access only to the particular department with which they have business. As the badge-authorized person continues beyond the gate, he approaches a rather nondescript, gray, seven-level headquarters building. Outside the building is a large statue of Nathan Hale . . . not only to honor an early American hero, but a rather whimsical and subtle acknowledgment that those who work here are in the business of spying.

Senator Josh Kelly stopped at the gate as a uniformed guard approached his car.

"I'm Senator Kelly," Josh said.

"May I see some identification, please?" the guard asked.

"Are you saying that you don't recognize me?" Kelly asked, a little put out by the request.

"Identification, please," the guard repeated.

Kelly showed him his driver's license and his Senate ID card. The guard took both the license and the card back to the guardhouse where he tapped a few keys into a computer.

"Senator, look at the green square please," the guard said over a small speaker.

Kelly looked at it and saw a little red light blink. A few seconds later the guard returned to the car, bringing not only the driver's license and Senate ID card, but a yellow badge. As Kelly looked at the badge, he saw that it already had his photo, along with his name, origin, and destination. At the bottom of the badge was a bar code of some sort.

"Please put the badge on now and wear it, conspicuously, for the whole time you are here," the guard said.

"Where do I go?" Kelly asked.

"Proceed to parking area C," the guard said. "Enter through the main door, then take the elevator to the fourth floor. Turn right as you exit the elevator on the fourth floor. Go to room 414. Do not go anywhere else. Should you attempt to go anywhere else, alarms will be activated and you will be arrested."

"I'm a United States Senator," Kelly said.

"Do not got anywhere other than your place of authorization," the guard repeated. "If you do, you will be arrested."

Kelly glared at the guard, but he attached the badge to his jacket lapel, just under the small Purple Heart pin. When the guard opened the gate, he drove straight ahead.

Once inside the building, Kelly followed the guard's instructions to the letter. When he reached the door to room 414, it opened before he could open it. A tall, balding man with a puffy red face and wire-rim glasses met him.

"Senator Kelly, thank you for coming."

"You are Mark Roberts?"

"Yes. Come in, please."

Kelly followed Roberts into the room, which was a conference room with black walls. At first he thought the walls were painted black, but as he looked closer he saw that they were covered with some sort of fabric. The ceiling was also black, covered with the same material, and embedded with several lights. Only one bank of the lights were on now, and the room seemed plenty bright enough. He wondered how bright it would be if all the lights were burning.

"Stand there, please," Roberts said, pointing to a specific spot.

"Stand here? Why?"

Roberts stepped to the other side of the table and pressed a button. Kelly was aware of a green bar of light that passed up and down his body, quickly. Oddly, it reminded him of the light one could sometimes see under the cover of a copy machine as it made a copy.

"Please turn off your cell phone and place it on the table," Roberts said.

"I'm expecting a call."

"You won't get it while you are in here. No outside signal can come in or leave."

"Then why must I turn the phone off?"

"Please do it, Senator."

Kelly did as he was instructed.

"And now your recorder."

"I beg your pardon?"

"Your recorder. Hand it to me, please."

"How did you know . . ." Kelly paused for a second,

then reached into his inside jacket pocket and removed a very small digital recorder. He held it for a moment before handing it over.

"I don't like to take meetings with people without having a record of those meetings. I'm sure you can understand that someone in my position could be very vulnerable if misinformation was put out."

"I do understand," Roberts said.

Kelly smiled and put the recorder back in his pocket. "I thought you might."

"I'll show you out," Robert said.

"What?"

"If you insist on keeping the recorder, I'm afraid there will be no meeting. I'll show you out."

"No, no, wait," Kelly said. Again he pulled out his recorder, this time handing it over. "All right, you win."

"Good."

Roberts took the recorder, removed the battery, then put it on the table in front of him. He gestured toward a chair. "Have a seat, Senator."

Kelly sat in the proffered chair.

"Look," Kelly said. "I don't appreciate being treated like a . . . a spy. I remind you that you are the one who contacted me."

"Indeed I did, Senator, as soon as I found out about your hearings on clandestine activities in Colombia."

"They weren't actually hearings, it would have taken a meeting of the full committee to be a hearing."

"Yes, I know," Roberts said. "Whatever they were, I believe they have provided us with an opportunity to help each other."

"Help each other?"

"Yes."

Kelly smiled. This was more to his liking. Mark Roberts wanted something from him, and he had many years of dealing with people who wanted something from him. That put him back in a position of authority.

"All right, what do you have for me?" Kelly asked.

"The Code Name Team."

Kelly shook his head. "I know all about the Code Name Team. They are led by someone called John Barrone. They are a group of mercenaries, funded by private citizens. They have nothing to do with the government."

"What if I told you that they are in Colombia as a black ops, authorized by the CIA?" Roberts asked.

"Do you know that for a fact? Can you prove it?"

"Yes and no," Roberts replied.

"What do you mean, yes and no?"

"Yes, I know it for a fact. But, no, I can't prove it."

"Why are you telling me this, if it isn't actionable?" Kelly asked.

"It is actionable," Roberts insisted. "If you have the balls to act on it."

Kelly sat there for a long moment, drumming his fingers on the table.

"Now I need to ask you if you are wired," he said.

"I'm not."

"Mind if I look around?"

"Be my guest. I chose this room because it's secure."

Kelly looked around the room. There was a screen of some sort, flush with the table, in front of Roberts, but nothing that looked like a microphone. There were no telephones in the room. Leaning down, Kelly looked under the table, but saw nothing. There were only two chairs, both clean. He pointed to the screen in front of Roberts. "What is that?"

"It's a body scanner," Roberts replied. "That's how I knew about your recorder. Would you like me to demonstrate it for you?"

"Yes."

Roberts got up and walked around to stand in the same place he had directed Kelly to stand in a moment earlier.

"Push the button beside the screen, then monitor the screen," Roberts said.

Kelly did so and in his peripheral vision saw the little green bar of light travel down Roberts's body. He looked at the screen.

"Son of a bitch!" he said in surprise.

On the screen were four images of Roberts, front, back, and each side. His billfold, car keys, a few coins, the outline of his clothes, were visible as transparent objects. Beyond the clothes, the images of his body were absolutely nude . . . not the shadows of MRI or X-ray . . . but nude in full-flesh color, just as if Roberts had taken off his clothes.

"Satisfied?" Roberts asked.

"Son of a bitch!" Kelly said again. "I'll bet you enjoy scanning the women."

Roberts smiled. "It has its compensations," he said. He came back around the table, Kelly returned to his side, and they both took their seats.

"Now, I will ask my question again," Roberts said. "Do you have the balls to deal with this?"

"Before I answer that, I'd like to know what your position is," Kelly said. "You want something from me. What is it?"

Roberts took off his glasses and polished them with his tie.

"You were in Vietnam," Roberts said.

"Yes, I got the Purple Heart and—"

"I know how you got your Purple Heart, Senator, you were in the USARV," Roberts said, dismissively.

"Uh, yes. United States Army, Vietnam."

"Do you recall Operation Phoenix?"

"Yes, of course I do. It was an operation whereby Americans murdered some twenty thousand Vietnamese civilians. According to one source I read, it was the most systematic, politically motivated, mass-murder project since Hitler and World War Two."

"The true number was closer to forty thousand," Roberts said. "And it wasn't murder, it was selective weeding of Communists from South Vietnam's infrastructure. If the bleeding-heart liberals hadn't found out about it, and put a stop to it, we would have won the war."

"We? You were a part of the Phoenix operation?"

"Yes," Roberts said. He put his glasses on, then leaned back in his chair and folded his arms across his chest. "I was more than a part of it, I was one of the architects of the project."

"That's interesting, but what does that have to do with the Code Name Team?"

"Several years ago, I was recommended for promotion to the position of director of operations. That would have put me on track to become deputy director, which is as high as you can go in the career field. The director had me vetted . . . just routine, he said. Two men investigated me: John Barrone and Harley Thomas."

Roberts leaned forward and put his arms on the table. "Those bastards were nothing but pups. Neither one of them had even been around during the Vietnam War. They had no idea what we were facing then. But when they discovered my association with the Phoenix program, they reported on it to the director.

"The director was a liberal pussy, appointed by a liberal pussy president. Needless to say, I didn't get my promotion. In fact, Harley Thomas has the job today that I was trying to get then. Now they have me stuck down in some paper-shuffling job, just waiting out the time for my retirement."

"Uh, look, Roberts, I'm sorry about that, but there's really nothing I can do about it now."

"Did I ask you to do anything about that?" Roberts snapped with a dismissive wave of his hand.

"Well, no, not directly, but I thought—"

"The two men who are most responsible for what happened to me are up to their assholes in what's going on down in Colombia. Harley is running a black ops, so deep that nobody else in the Company knows about it. And he is running it through Barrone and the Code Name Team."

"If nobody in the Company knows about it, how do you know about it?"

"I have a source," Roberts said without being specific. "Now, I ask you again, do you have the balls to do what it takes to rid yourself of this problem?"

"I have the balls," Kelly said. "Damn right, I have the balls."

"I know where their safe house is."

"How do you know?"

"As I said, Senator, I have a source. An inside source."

"Okay, so you tell me where the safe house is, what do I do then?"

"You eradicate the problem."

"How?"

"The Code Name Team has been involved in two operations down there. The first one was a drug factory. That was damn near disastrous for them. The second was the house of Gilberto Escobar. That was much more successful for them, they got away with around five million dollars. I don't know about you, Senator, but to me that sounds like they are trying to muscle in on the drug business there and start their own cartel."

"Damn, it does at that, doesn't it?"

"As I said, I know where their safe house is. If someone . . . like, say, a United States Senator . . . went to the right Colombian official, I believe you could get a military unit to act against their safe house."

"Act against?"

"Yes."

Kelly shook his head. "No, I can't do that. That would have to come from someone in the administration . . . the State Department, or the Department of Justice. I couldn't do that as a U.S. Senator."

"All I can do is lay it out for you, Senator. Like I said, you would have to have a pair of balls to pull it off."

"But how would I do it?"

"I tell you what, you give me an official request from the Senate Foreign Relations Committee to look into this operation. I'll take care of the rest."

"I can't even do that. That would have to come from the chairman," Kelly said.

"You are the ranking member. Can't you request it from him, just on suspicion?"

Kelly shook his head. "Not without a lot of concrete evidence that my suspicions are valid."

Roberts smiled. "Then that's your answer. As ranking member, what you are doing is undertaking a personal investigation to find the evidence you need to bring it to him. Under those circumstances, you can ask me to look into it for you."

Kelly nodded, and returned Roberts's smile. "Yes," he said. "Yes, as ranking member, I can ask that you look into my suspicions to see if they justify action by the chairman."

"I'll get right on it," Roberts said.

Bogota, Colombia

When Special Agent Lucas Tyreen of the U.S. Drug Enforcement Agency got the operational order from his next higher, he read it with some surprise. To eliminate with extreme prejudice meant to kill.

> *Information has come to light that a group of highly skilled and exceptionally dangerous individuals, calling themselves the Code Name Team, are now operating in Colombia. Reliable sources indicate that the Code Name Team is responsible for two recent, high-profile attacks on the drug cartel, resulting in the theft of a great deal of money.*
>
> *We believe these former, and now rogue, intelligence and security agents intend to establish their own drug cartel in Colombia.*
>
> *Such an operation would be extremely detrimental to the U.S. Government for two reasons. One, it would impact upon our already strained drug enforcement resources. Also, because there is a quasi connection between the Code Name Team and the U.S. Government, their freelance and unchecked observations could cause irreparable damage to the relations between the U.S. and Colombia.*
>
> *Accordingly, you are hereby instructed to locate and to eliminate with extreme prejudice the following named American nationals, known to be operating in Colombia: JOHN BARRONE, JENIFER BARNES, LINDA MARSH, MIKE ROJAS, CHRIS FARMER, PAUL BREWER, and DON YEE.*

The first thing Tryeen did was ask for verification of the order. The order was verified, not only by his next higher, but also by the CIA.

"By what means am I to accomplish this task?" he asked.

"We have arranged for you to meet with the minister of interior and justice," Tyreen was told.

As a result of those arrangements, Tyreen was now sitting on a brown leather couch in the office of the minister of interior and justice. He picked up a little crystal ball and turned it to watch the snow fall on the miniature Alpine village inside. He was waiting, while Minister Sabas de la Vega spoke on the phone.

"*Sí, gracias,*" de la Vega said as he hung up.

Tyreen set the crystal ball down as de la Vega came back over to the seating area. De la Vega sat down in a chair across from the sofa. "That was Andres Velasco, the minister of defense," he said. "He has just authorized use of the Ninth Fusilier Battalion against the Americans known as the Code Name Team. And, because it involves American nationals, he has officially asked you to go along on the operation."

"Are you and your government certain that the Americans are actually trying to set up their own drug cartel?"

De la Vega reached for a manila folder and picked it up, then opened it and began looking at the documents inside.

"I have all the information you need right here," he said. "We have statements from the CIA, as well as an unofficial request from the ranking member of the Senate Foreign Relations Committee, to look into it."

"An unofficial request," Tyreen said.

"Call it a courtesy request."

"Well, my next higher told me to offer you every cooperation, so I guess you can count me in."

"Tell me about this Code Name Team. Have you ever heard of them?"

"Yes, I have. That's why I'm having a hard time believing that they have gone rogue."

"Are they a part of your government?"

"No. That is, I don't think so. Certainly not if they are involved as you say they are. Actually, they've done some very good things in the past. For example, they rescued Senator Clayton from a bunch of terrorists a few years ago." Tyreen chuckled. "Of course, I guess your political stripe would determine whether or not that was actually a good thing. They are made up of ex-agents and officers."

"What went wrong, I wonder?" de la Vega asked.

"Who knows?" Tyreen replied. "When people are way out on the edge like that . . . sometimes they fall off. And you say you've located their safe house?"

"Yes."

"I can't imagine them being so careless as to let you find them like that. You are sure of your information?"

"Yes, I'm very sure. I've gotten my information from an unimpeachable source."

"Unimpeachable?" Tyreen repeated.

"Yes."

The minister of justice wrote something on a piece of paper, then handed it to Tyreen. "Show this to Major Santos Marina of the Ninth Fusiliers Battalion. This will allow you to accompany him and, it is to be hoped, prevent an international incident."

"Thanks," Tyreen said.

"Good luck," de la Vega said, standing along with Tyreen and reaching out to shake his hand.

With the authorizing orders in his hand, Tyreen left the offices of the Ministry of Interior and Justice and headed for the headquarters of the Ninth Fusiliers.

Chapter 17

"Do you know this place?" Tyreen asked, showing an address to Major Santos Marina.

"*Sí*, I know the place. It is a very expensive house, senor. You are sure that the people we are after are here in this place?"

"I'm told the source is very reliable."

"What is your source?"

"I could tell you that," Tyreen said. "But then I would have to kill you."

"*Qué?*" Marina responded in surprise.

"It is a joke," Tyreen said.

"Oh, a joke. Yes, it is very funny," Major Marina said in a way that indicated he didn't think it was funny at all.

"Trust me, it has all been laid out for us by your government and mine," Tyree said.

"Good, good, then we will have no trouble."

Tyreen stroked his chin and shook his head. "Oh, I wouldn't say that, Major. From all I've been able to ascertain about these people, they are extremely skilled at what they do."

"So are my brave, young soldiers," Major Marina replied. "We have fought many battles with the FARC.

I think we will have no problem with a few American civilians."

"I hope you are right," Tyreen said. "I just hope you are right."

Code Name Safe House, Cali, Colombia

The Code Name Team was on the veranda of the house they had rented for the duration. Paul had prepared barbecued shrimp for them, and bowls of the delicacy were scattered around. Along with the shrimp they were enjoying the champagne Fidel had given them.

"Damn, this is good stuff," Chris said. "I'd pay five hundred dollars a bottle for it any day."

"Sure you would," John said sarcastically. He took a sip. "But it is damn good."

"What was the final count again?" Linda asked.

"Five million four hundred and sixty thousand dollars," Don said.

"Yes, well, like Senator Dirksen once said, a million here and a million there and pretty soon you're talking about real money," Chris said.

John chuckled. "Yeah, only that was billions with a *b* he was talking about."

"Ah, well, then we are still in the pauper stage, aren't we?"

"We are according to the intel we got before we left the States," John said. "Mendoza is supposed to have half a billion dollars in drug money stashed away somewhere."

"You think we'll find it?" Linda asked.

"We're damn sure going to give it a look," John replied.

"Hey, guys, look at this," Jennifer said, pointing toward the TV screen. The TV was on, but the sound had been muted.

"That's Senator Kelly," Linda said. "What is he doing, holding a press conference?"

John shook his head. "No, it looks more like a committee hearing. Turn it up, Don."

Don picked up the remote that was right beside him and pointed it at the TV.

". . . cannot simply close our eyes to the hopes and aspirations of a people to create an environment where they can live in freedom and economic independence," Kelly was saying. "I now call Lui Mendoza, president designate of the emerging nation of Pangea."

Amid the flash of bulbs, and the grinding sound of film being advanced, reporters and photographers buzzed with interest as Mendoza took the stand.

"President Mendoza," Kelly said, "as this is not an official hearing, and you are not an American citizen, we will forgo the swearing in, trusting instead upon your honor as chief executive of a new nation."

"Honor?" Chris said angrily, speaking to the screen. "What the hell makes him think that son of a bitch even recognizes the word *honor*, let alone possesses it?"

"Well, you've put your finger on it," John said. "Kelly doesn't understand the concept of honor himself. How would he recognize it in anyone else?"

"And now, President Mendoza, I understand you have an opening statement you would like to read to the committee."

"Yes," Mendoza replied. Opening a folder, he began to read.

"Almost two hundred years ago, the great hero Simon Bolivar tried valiantly to carry out a bourgeois-democratic revolution in Colombia, Venezuela, and Ecuador, but the cowardly and unpatriotic bourgeoisie would not cooperate. Today, I have taken the torch from Bolivar and . . ."

"Turn that shit off!" John said.

Don turned off the TV.

Normandia District of Cali

It was midafternoon when the Ninth Fusilier Battalion moved into position at the edge of the woods. Major Marina moved a branch to one side and studied the house through his binoculars.

"Do you see anyone?" Tyreen asked.

"There seems to be some movement in the lower right part of the house," Marina said, handing the binoculars over to Tyreen. "Would you care to take a look?"

Tyreen looked through the binoculars and saw a woman standing near the window. She was tall, with dark hair, and even from here, he could tell that she was a beautiful woman. For a moment he felt a sense of hesitancy, the kind of hesitancy anyone would have about destroying something beautiful. He stared at her for a long moment, then lowered the glasses and handed them back to Marina.

"That's them, all right," he said.

"Shall we call out to them, announce that we have them surrounded and call for their surrender?"

Tyreen shook his head. "No," he said. "Commence the attack."

"But, surely, you intend to offer them the chance of surrender?" Major Marina said. "After all, it is the only decent thing to do."

"The people in that house have killed many men, women, and children, not just in Colombia, not just in America, but all over the world," Tyreen said. "We cannot take a chance on their escaping. Commence the attack."

"Very well," Marina said. Quickly, he shouted orders to his men. Crew-served machine guns were put into place, a mortar crew got ready to set up their tube and baseplate, the soldiers slipped magazines into the receivers of their weapons, then operated the bolt levers and looked expectantly toward Marina, awaiting his order.

Marina looked at Tyreen, as if offering him one last time to change his mind, but Marina continued to stare at the house, consciously avoiding Tyreen.

Marina held his hand up.

Nearby, the birds were singing.

Overhead, far, far removed from the drama about to play out below, an airliner left a white contrail in the cold stratosphere.

Marina brought his hand down, sharply.

"*Comience el ataque!*" he shouted.

Inside the safe house

Suddenly the windows shattered and they could hear the sound of firing as bullets sprayed into the house. The Code Name Team hit the floor, then began scooting on their bellies to get closer to the walls for the protection they offered.

A rocket-propelled grenade streamed in and detonated right in front of the television. The TV was completely destroyed.

"Is anyone hit?" John shouted. "Jennifer, Linda, Chris, Paul, Don, Mike . . . sound off!"

"I'm okay," Jennifer called back. One by one the others responded as well.

More bullets slammed into the house, everyone

staying down on the floor. They crawled over to the window, reaching a position to look out and return fire. Though, as they had only pistols, they were at a distinct disadvantage.

John saw a series of winking lights on the edge of the nearby tree line, followed almost immediately by more bullets slamming into the house.

"Damn!" Chris said. "Whoever that is, they aren't playing around. That's a crew-served weapon."

Eight men came running out of the tree line and all took up positions behind an outcropping of rocks. From their improved position, they began firing as well, increasing the volume of bullets that were coming into the house. Four more men ran out to join them. One of them was carrying a mortar tube, a second was carrying the baseplate. The other two men were carrying mortar ammunition.

"Son of a bitch," Mike said. "They've got a mortar."

It took less than a minute for the mortar to be set up. Then they heard it fire, watched the plume of smoke as the round left the tube and climbed high into the sky, only to come plunging back down. It burst in the lawn about ten yards in front of the house.

One of the men raised himself up and looked at the house through binoculars.

"Shoot him," John called. "If we all shoot, one of us might hit him."

All fired their pistols and the man fell back, his binoculars tumbling through the air.

"Ha! I got him!" Don shouted in glee.

"You got him?" Linda asked.

"Well, yeah, didn't you see him fall?"

The others laughed, despite the current situation.

The mortar fired a second time, and this time it didn't miss. The round plunged down through the roof of the house and exploded upstairs. Though none of the shrapnel penetrated to the lower level, a lot of plaster did fall down.

The next rocket-propelled grenade did more, again bursting inside the great room. This time the shrapnel whizzed and whistled about them.

"Uhnn!" Mike said, falling back.

"John, Mike's hit!" Paul said.

"How bad?" John asked anxiously.

Paul looked at his wound. "Oh, shit," he said, in a strained voice.

Looking over toward Paul, John saw Mike lying on his stomach.

"Mike?" John shouted, hurrying to him. He turned Mike over, then looked away.

There was a big hole in Mike's chest, right over his heart. Mike's eyes were open, but already clouding over.

"Oh, Jesus," John said quietly.

"How bad is it?" Linda asked.

"He's . . . he's dead," John said, barely able to say the words.

Another mortar round crashed into the house, this one coming down through the ceiling to explode on the ground floor.

"John, we've got to get out of here, or they're going to bring this whole house down on us," Chris said.

"Yeah, I know."

"The problem is, how?" Linda asked. "They've got our only way out blocked."

"Then we go that way," John said. He pointed toward the back of the house.

"Oh no, wait a minute," Don said, shaking his head. "What do you mean we go that way? There *is* no that way!"

"That's the only way we can go."

"But it's straight down!" Don said.

"True."

"Like, five hundred feet or so."

"What are you worried about, Don? Aren't you a qualified flyer?"

"Yes," Don said. "With a helicopter or an airplane. Not with my arms." He flapped them a couple of times.

"Well then, I guess you'd better climb, hadn't you?" John said.

"What about the money?" Jennifer asked. "We won't be able to take it with us."

"Burn it," John said.

"Burn it?" the others asked, as one.

"Jennifer's right. We can't take it with us. Everyone grab as many packets as you can stick in your pockets or pants, then, Jennifer, rig a thermite device to burn the rest."

"Son of a bitch," Chris said, shaking his head. "I've had some wild-assed dreams in my life, but burning five million dollars wasn't one of them."

The bullets continued to pop and zing through the house as Jennifer set the thermite devices.

"Okay!" she shouted. "They're ready!"

"Burn 'em!" John shouted.

Jennifer touched a button on a device that looked somewhat like a TV remote, and there was a brilliant flash of a fireball, followed by flames and rolling smoke as the stack of bills began to burn.

"Let's get out of here!" John shouted. "Chris, you and Paul keep Don between you!"

"John, what are we going to do about Mike?" Linda asked. "We can't just leave him here."

"We'll take him," John said.

"Take him? What do you mean, take him?" Don said. "We can't carry him down the side of a cliff."

"Who said we had to—" John started to reply, but his words were cut short by the crashing of another mortar shell. This one plunged all the way down into the great room before it exploded.

"John!" Linda shouted.

If John answered her, his reply was lost in the cacophony of the collapsing and burning house.

The house burned furiously, and the fire spread rapidly.

Tyreen picked through the smoldering rubble with Major Santos and his soldiers.

"They are dead, senor," Santos said.

"How do you know they are dead? Have we found any bodies?"

"No, senor, but we were watching the house very closely and no one got out. Do you think anyone could have lived through this?"

"I suppose not," Tyreen said.

"Major," one of the soldiers called, "I have found something."

"Well, finally," Tyreen said, starting toward the soldier with the major. "What is it? A body?"

The soldier was holding a one-hundred-dollar bill.

"You called us over for this?" Tyreen asked, disappointed that it wasn't proof of death.

"Where did you find it?" Major Santos asked.

"Here," the soldier said, pointing.

There, near an overturned marble table that was seared by the flames, was a large pile of blackened residue. A closer examination of the residue indicated that it was probably stacks of money, though they were all burned to a cinder, and when a few of the soldiers began picking them up, looking for usable money, the little packets crumbled into fine black powder.

"*Mierda Santa,* how much money do you think is here?" Major Santos asked.

"A lot," Tyreen said. "Several million dollars."

"Well, that should prove that they died in the fire," Major Santos said. "I do not believe they would have left several million dollars behind."

"No, I don't either," Tyreen said. He walked away from the pile of blackened rubble, then used his satellite phone to make a call.

"Operations," a voice said at the other end.

"This is Tyreen. Mission accomplished," he said. He paused for a second, then added, "With extreme prejudice."

Chapter 18

The story had been carried on all the major networks, and was repeated every half hour on the cable news networks. The big TV screen in the den was on and Wagner was watching it, along with Lana Henry and Bob Garrett, the only two members of the team who had not gone to Colombia. Lana was wiping her eyes with her handkerchief.

A young, intense newscaster was reporting the story.

"Our top story comes to us from the jungles of Colombia. There, seven Americans were killed in a shoot-out with members of the Colombian military. The Americans have not been identified yet, but were said to be members of a team of mercenaries calling themselves the Code Name Team.

"Our viewers may remember the Code Name Team as ones who made a daring rescue of Senator Harriet Clayton a few years ago, when she was being held by terrorists. Kyle Roach has that story. Kyle?"

The scene switched to another young man, this one standing alongside Harriet Clayton.

"Brian, with me is Senator Harriet Clayton who, as you said, was rescued a few years ago by the Code Name Team. Senator Clayton, your thoughts on the news?" He held the microphone in front of Harriet.

"I was saddened by the news. As you know, they did rescue me, at great peril to their own lives. But they were all brave, skilled, and dedicated men and women."

"And yet, they were mercenaries," Kyle said. "Cowboys, some might say. How do you reconcile your admiration for them with the fact that you have spent your entire political career opposing military adventure?"

"I'm not saying I approve of them, or of whatever it is they were doing down in Colombia. My admiration of them is limited to an appreciation for their skill and bravery, and also for the fact that they saved my life." Harriet flashed a practiced smile. "I can have a great deal of admiration for anyone who saves my life."

Kyle chuckled. "I suppose you can at that," he said. "Back to you, Brian."

The picture returned to the news studio, where, once again, Brian stared earnestly into the camera.

"Thank you, Kyle. We go now to St. Louis where Senator Josh Kelly is set to deliver a speech tonight at Washington University. With Senator Kelly is Steve Cantrell. Steve?"

A wide shot showed the Arch, then it tightened on reporter Steve Cantrell.

"Brian, as we have reported, Senator Kelly is advocating U.S. recognition for the new nation of Pangea, once it comes into being. And to help drum up support for that position, he is on a nationwide speaking tour, speaking tonight at the prestigious Washington University in St. Louis. I asked him, just a few minutes ago, what his reaction was to the news that several American mercenaries had been killed in Colombia, and this was his response."

"Steve, some are saying that these men and

women of this so-called Code Name Team were people of ideals, that somehow by being down here they were fighting for freedom.

"That is perfect nonsense. They were down here for two reasons. One reason was an attempt to stop a group of people from declaring their independence. And the other was related to the first. They were there to consolidate their own positions within the drug culture, and they felt that preventing the people of Pangea from declaring their independence was the best way to do that."

"But, Senator, doesn't that fly in the face of what we know about them?"

"I don't know. What do we know about them?" Kelly replied.

"Well, we know they rescued Senator Clayton a few years ago when she—"

"Yes, yes, we've heard all about that," Kelly said. "Interesting, though, that few people mention the very healthy reward that was paid for her safe return."

"So you are saying that their mission to save Senator Clayton was motivated, not by idealism, but by money?"

"Exactly. Look at why they were in Colombia. They were there hoping to take advantage of the transition to the new nation of Pangea by staking out their claim on the drug market."

"Some have suggested that they were there to help shore up the Free Colombia Brigade, a movement that hoped to stop the establishment of Pangea."

"If that is true, they were doing it for whatever financial reward they could gain by their support," Kelly said. I believe that we owe the Colombian Army a debt of gratitude for taking care of them. They were what you might call a loose cannon on the deck of American diplomacy." Kelly looked right into the camera so he could speak directly to the American people.

"This is one more reason why we should support the efforts of the Pangean people to establish their own nation . . . for only then, working hand in hand with President Mendoza, will we be able to win this war against drugs, once and for all. So I'm asking all of you to . . ."

"I don't give a rat's ass what you are asking us all to do," Wagner said, picking up the remote and turning off the TV.

"We don't know that they are dead," Bob Garrett said. Bob was in his middle forties. For the last fifteen years before he joined the Code Name Team, he had worked for the National Security Agency. And for five years before that, he had worked for the CIA. Bob's most useful talent was the fact that he could blend, quickly, into any crowd and had an almost chameleon-like ability to adapt his speech patterns and body language to fit those around him.

"Then why haven't we heard from them?" Lana asked.

"I don't know," Bob admitted. "I just know that I've been with them . . . and you have too . . . in a lot of tight spots before. I'm just not ready to give up on them yet."

"I'm not either," Lana said. "But I would be lying to you if I told you I wasn't worried."

Lana was a very attractive woman in her mid-thirties who spent ten years with the Bureau of Alcohol, Tobacco, and Firearms. Like Linda Marsh, Lana was a martial arts expert.

"I'll try and get through to them again," Wagner said. "It's not like them to stay out of touch for so long. There must be a good reason for it."

Buenaventura, Colombia, Mendoza's estate

Mendoza's house, which he had already designated as the *Palacio del Presidente,* was on the west end of Buenaventura. It was surrounded by a twelve-foot-high wall built of brick and concrete. There were only two ways into the compound, one on the east side, which was the front, and another on the north. The west side had no entrances, for the only approach was by the sea.

Even though Pangea was not yet an independent nation, the new flag of Pangea—orange, with a white circle in the middle of a black St. Andrews cross, and a black, four-pointed star in the white circle—flew from flagstaffs at every corner of the palace grounds.

Every building within two blocks of the palace had been razed, by order of El Presidente-for-Life Mendoza. This draconian measure was to prevent any building from supplying a place from which a sniper could assassinate Mendoza. And the order was carried out, even though Mendoza was not yet the president.

The soldiers at the east gate came to attention as the big black Cadillac rolled through. Mendoza, freshly returned from his visit to the United States, was in the backseat of the car, wearing one of the uniforms he had had designed and tailor-made for him while he was in New York.

Gato Valdez, who had come back from New York two days earlier to prepare for Mendoza's return, met him under the portico, and after the back door of the car was opened, Mendoza stepped out.

"How do you like it?" he asked, turning once to show off the uniform.

The uniform was olive green, with a black-lined orange stripe down each pant leg. There was a large triangular, fold-back lapel across his chest. It was also orange, though it was filled with a dozen or so medals. His epaulets were gold braid, with a golden-fringed tassel hanging down from the right one.

"*Magnifico. Absolutamente magnifico,*" Gato said enthusiastically.

"I think my people will appreciate it as well," Mendoza said.

Mendoza went inside, to his office, with Gato following behind him.

"Have you heard the news, El Presidente?" Gato asked.

"What news is that?"

"The Code Name Team. They are all dead."

"Yes, it has been on television and in the newspapers. But how do we know they are dead? Have you, with your own eyes, seen the dead bodies of these people?"

"Well, no, *Excelencia.* But it has been in the news," Gato said.

"I know it has been in the news, *idiota,*" Mendoza snapped. "I asked if you had seen the bodies with your own eyes.

"No, *Excelencia,*" Gato said, stung by the appellation. "But Major Marin took pictures taken of the house where they were staying. Pictures that have not been seen on TV. I have the tape queued up if you would care to view it."

"*Sí,* I will watch," Mendoza replied.

By now they were in Mendoza's office, and as soon as Mendoza settled onto the big leather sofa, Gato picked up the remote and turned on the TV and VCR.

"As you can see, the house was completely leveled, first by artillery, then by fire. The house was under constant surveillance and no one was seen leaving.

It would have been impossible for anyone to have remained in the house and survived.

"Seen here walking through the rubble of the De Soto Home are Major Santos and his executive officer, Captain Calvario."

There was a civilian with them as well, walking through the ashes, here bending over to pick up something, there kicking something aside. The narrator of the tape never mentioned the stranger, but Mendoza saw it at once.

"Who is that?" he asked.

"Who are you talking about?" Gato asked.

"Him," Mendoza said, pointing to the man in question. "The civilian."

Gato stopped the tape and stared at the picture for a while.

"Yes, who is that, do you know?"

"No."

"It's an American," Mendoza said.

"How can you be so sure?" Gato asked.

Mendoza didn't respond to Gato's question. Instead, he just glared at him. "What was that American civilian doing with Major Santos?"

"I don't know."

"Find out."

"*Sí, Excelencia.*"

"Oh, and the owner of that house? Manuel De Soto? Find him and bring him to me."

"*Sí.*"

Gato picked up the telephone as Mendoza left the room, then went upstairs to his bedroom. The room was redolent with the fragrance of Toujours Moi perfume.

She was lying in his bed, waiting for him. She was totally naked, and when she lifted her left arm in invitation, her left breast flattened, causing the nipple to be more pronounced.

"Have you been waiting long?" Mendoza asked as he started undoing the buttons on his tunic.

"I've been waiting so long that I started without you," Katy Correal said, in a low, throaty voice as her finger dipped back into the bush at the junction of her legs.

Cali, Colombia

Bob Garrett and Lana Henry were in Cali to continue Operation Rolling Thunder. Because they did not know whom to trust, they weeded their contact list down to only one name, and that was Viktor Marin. And they chose him because they knew, going in, that he was, in the words of the report they had on him, "anyone's ally who could pay the price."

What they were counting on was that they would be able to buy his loyalty.

The bicycle shop was quite busy when they arrived, and they were met by a boy of about sixteen.

"*Son usted turistas Américanos?*" the boy asked.

"*Sí,*" Bob answered. "Do you speak English? *Haga usted dice inglés?*"

The boy shook his head. "No."

"Viktor Marin. *Quiero hablar a Viktor Marin,*" Bob said.

"I am Viktor Marin," a tall, thin man with a bushy moustache and wire-rim glasses said, coming over to them then. "Do you have business with me?"

"We hope to do some business with you, yes," Bob said. "Is there some place we can talk?"

"What is there to talk about?" Marin asked.

"Will this let me choose the subject?" Bob asked, handing Marin ten one-hundred-dollar bills.

Marin took the money and put it in his pocket. "For this, I will tell you my prices for other services," he said.

Bob snorted a laugh. "Yeah, I thought as much. But for one thousand dollars, I expect a more comfortable and private place to talk than standing in the middle of a bicycle shop."

"Across the street is a coffeehouse," Marin said. "I am a friend with the owner. Sometimes he lets me use a back room of his establishment if I wish to talk privately."

"Sounds like a good idea," Bob said.

Bob and Lana followed Marin across the street, picking their way through bicyclists, motorbikes, and vintage cars. An old woman sat on the sidewalk in front of the coffeehouse, surrounded by an array of straw hats for sale. A man and woman, obviously American, were looking at the hats, trying them on one at a time.

"Oh, Ben, look at this one," the woman said, picking up a wide-brimmed hat of bright red. This one is me, don't you think?"

"Absolutely," Ben said.

"No, maybe this one."

The woman put down the red hat and picked up another, but the old lady who was selling them continued to stare straight ahead, making no effort to sell, showing no reaction whatever to their picking through her wares.

The coffeehouse catered only to the locals, or to the tourists who wanted an authentic touch of local color. There were half a dozen tables, many on uneven legs, compensated for by little blocks of wood or several folds of paper underneath the short leg.

The floor was unpainted wide planking, the walls were flyblown and covered with various photos and advertising flyers. There was also a six-year-old calendar, its position earned by the photograph of a very attractive young woman.

"That is Pablo's daughter," Marin said, when he saw that Lana was looking with curiosity at the old calendar.

"She is very pretty," Lana replied.

"Yes, she is. Pablo, we will talk in the back room," Marin called out.

"Coffee?" Pablo replied.

"*Sí.*"

There was only one table in the back room, and the room was barely large enough to contain it. Marin motioned toward it, and Bob and Lana sat down. They sat in such a way as to cover each other's backs and Marin noticed it, but he didn't say anything about it.

"What subject do you wish to talk about?" Marin asked after he was seated at the table with them.

"We have reason to believe that you recently did business with some of our friends," Bob said.

"I do business with many people," Marin said. "When tourists come to Cali, a bicycle is a good way to get around and see the sights."

"This wasn't bicycle business," Bob said.

Marin said nothing.

"Look, I gave you one thousand dollars to hold a conversation with me," Bob said. "I would hope that the one thousand dollars would buy some honesty."

"It will buy honesty, senor," Marin said. "But if you want more than honesty, it will cost you more."

"I am willing to pay more, much more, if you can provide some real information."

"How much more will you pay for information?" Marin asked.

"I will pay what the information is worth, as long as it is the truth."

"What do you want to know?"

"There are news reports that our friends, the ones you did business with, were recently killed."

"You are talking about the American mercenaries who came down here to rob the drug cartel?"

"They—" Lana started to say, but Bob recognized the angry tone in her voice so he cut her off before she could go any further.

"Yes," Bob said. "Those are the people we are asking about."

"What's there to ask? They were killed."

"Were the bodies found?"

"They burned up when the house burned."

"Come on, Senor Marin, you know that the bodies wouldn't have been completely consumed in a house fire. There would be something left."

Marin drummed his fingers on the table for a moment.

"I might be able to take you somewhere," he finally said. "You can find something out there, maybe."

"Where?"

"Some place," Marin said.

"For a price?"

"*Sí*, for a price."

"How much?"

"It will be expensive, senor. Expensive, and dangerous."

"How much?" Bob asked again.

"Ten thousand dollars, maybe."

Bob whistled. "That's a lot of money."

"As I said, senor, it will be dangerous. You do not mind this, because you want the information about your friends. But it will also be dangerous for me, and I have nothing to gain by putting myself in such danger. So I must charge you for it."

"All right," Bob said. "I'll pay the ten thousand dollars."

"You understand that I am only going to take you where you will be able to find out the truth," Marin said. "I think, maybe, you will not like the truth."

"Right now, the truth is all we are looking for," Bob said.

"When do you want to go?"

"Now," Bob said. "We want to go now."

Marin held out his hand, palm up. "Give me the ten thousand dollars," he said.

"How far is this place?"

"It is a long way from here. Maybe one hundred miles."

"You will furnish the transportation?"

"*Sí.*"

"All right. I will give you five thousand dollars now, and the other five thousand when we get to where we are going."

"You will have the money with you?"

"Yes."

"Then it is foolish for you not to pay it all to me now. How do you know I will not kill you and take the other five thousand dollars, once we have started?" Marin asked.

"I don't know that," Bob said. He smiled. "But on the other hand, you don't know that I won't kill you and take back the money I have already given you."

"Under the table, senor, I have a gun pointed at you. I could kill you right now, I think."

"Do it," Bob said.

Marin got a surprised look on his face. "*Qué?*"

"Both of us have guns pointed at you," Bob said.

"If you kill one of us now, the other will kill you. Go ahead, pull the trigger."

An uneasy smile spread across Marin's face, and he brought his gun up and put it on the table.

"I think maybe it is time we trust each other," Marin said.

"I think that is a good idea," Bob said, bringing his hands back up onto the table. Lana did so as well. It was obvious that neither of them had actually been holding a gun.

"Oh, senor, I think you pulled a very good trick on me," Marin said, laughing. "A very good trick."

Bob reached into his inside jacket pocket, and as he did so, the laughter left Marin's face, to be replaced by a quick look of fear. That look disappeared, however, when Bob pulled out a bound packet of money. He counted out fifty one-hundred-dollar bills, then slid them across the table to Marin.

"Let's get started," he said.

Chapter 19

Buenaventura, Colombia, Mendoza's estate

As Katy left the *Palacia del Presidente,* she met a gray Volvo coming into the estate. For just a moment her eyes made contact with those of the man in the backseat and she saw the fear in them. This, she knew, was Manuel De Soto, the man who owned the house where the Americans had been staying. She turned her head away, unable to confront the fear in his eyes.

Pueblo de Agua Buena

They drove into the plaza of a little town that looked like something from a travelogue, or a magazine advertisement, enticing one to "Come to picturesque Colombia."

"Look at this," Lana said. "I wouldn't be surprised if we didn't see Juan Valdez leading his donkey."

"Juan Valdez?" Marin said. "You are looking for someone named Juan Valdez?"

"It is a joke," Lana said, without attempting to explain about the classic TV coffee commercial.

The plaza was lined on three sides by cafés, the fourth side held down by a large church. There were

more carts than there were motor vehicles, so it wasn't
difficult to find a place for Marin to park his Rolls.

"We will eat our dinner, then get a hotel and stay
here tonight," Marin said.

"All right," Bob agreed.

They ate at a table on the sidewalk in front of one
of the cafés, enjoying the sights and sounds of the
town as they did so. A guitarist and two singers came
over to the table to serenade them, but Marin motioned for them to go away.

"No, wait," Lana called out to him. She handed
each of them a twenty-dollar bill. "Play something
nice," she invited.

The guitarist smiled and nodded. "*Gracias, gracias,*" he said as he stuck the money into his pocket.

The two men accompanying the guitar began a
rhythmic clacking of sticks, and shouting, "Ayiee, yi, yi,
yi, yi," in a musical tone. They were augmented by the
guitar, a steady, unwavering chord, through which
wound a haunting melody, like a golden thread woven
through a fine linen.

After several opening bars, the three began singing
in close harmony, and one of them started dancing,
clapping his hands over his head, tossing and twisting
and stomping in time with the music.

Later, the travelers took three rooms in the small
hotel. There were no phones in any of the rooms,
and the only bathroom was at the end of the hall.
That night, as they retired to their rooms, Lana
spoke quietly to Bob.

"How do we know he won't drive off during the
night?" she asked.

Smiling, Bob showed her the rotor cap. "He may
drive away, but it won't be in that Rolls."

* * *

"The car, it will not start," Marin said at breakfast the next morning.

"It will when I put the rotor cap back in," Bob said.

"You removed the rotor cap?"

"Yes."

"How can you not trust me?"

"How did you know the car wouldn't start, unless you already tried it?"

"I was merely going to move the car."

"About one hundred miles?"

"I am hurt that you did not trust me."

"Do something to earn my trust."

"I have," Marin said. "I have spoken to many people in this town, and they remember the Americans when they came through here. I think I know how to go from here."

"Good. As soon as we finish breakfast, I'll put the rotor cap back in, and we can get under way."

The sign on the suspension bridge read PELIGRO, "Danger."

"I am not going to drive across that bridge, senor," Marin said, stopping the car.

Bob looked at the long suspension bridge. It was sagging quite perceptibly to one side.

"Yeah, well, I can't say that I blame you," Bob said. "Any other way to get across this?"

"I am afraid it is a very long way before we can find another place to cross. And even if we find a way to cross, I do not know how to get back to the trail on the other side."

"Do you have any idea how far it is from here, to where we are going?"

"It is about ten more miles, I think."

"Then leave the car here. We'll walk."

"Senor, I will not leave my car here," Marin said. "It won't be here when I get back."

"He has a point, Bob," Lana said.

"All right, go back then. We'll go on alone."

"How will you get to the other side?"

"We'll walk across the bridge."

"It is not safe."

"We'll be careful."

"Ayiee," Marin said, wringing his hands. "*Todos los Americanos son locos.*"

"Nah, all Americans aren't crazy," Bob said. "We are just determined, that's all."

"I want the other five thousand dollars."

"No way. Our deal was ten thousand dollars for you to take us there. You haven't taken us there, so I want the five thousand back."

"But I brought you halfway," Marin insisted. "I brought you more than halfway."

"All right, I'll tell you what we will do. You keep your five thousand and I'll keep mine," Bob said. Bob and Lana got out of the car.

Marin stared at them for a long moment with barely controlled anger, then, making a disgusted gesture with his hand, he put the car in reverse and started backing down the road. Bob had been studying the road during the drive out. He knew Marin would have to go almost a mile before he could find a place to turn around.

Not until Marin was turned around and heading back toward Cali did he fish his satellite phone from the glove compartment and make a call.

"I left them at the bridge."

"Good."

"You will pay me as we agreed?"

"Yes."

On the trail with Bob and Lana

They had been walking for about half an hour when a car came onto the road from a very narrow trail. The car drew even with them and stopped. Bob had his hand on his pistol, but didn't draw it.

The window went down, revealing a very beautiful young woman.

"Are you lost?" she asked in English.

"Not exactly lost," Bob replied. "Just looking for something."

"What are you looking for?"

"I'll know when I find it."

The woman chuckled. "My, aren't we being secretive?" She stuck her hand through the open window. "My name is Katy Correal."

"Katy Correal?" Bob said.

"You say that as if you have heard my name," Katy replied.

"You were . . . friends . . . with Brian Skipper?"

The smile left her face, to be replaced by an expression of surprise.

"Yes. Yes, I was. How did you know that?"

"I just knew," Bob replied without going into detail. "My name is Bob Garrett. This is Lana Henry."

"Are you friends of John Barrone?" Katy asked.

"Yes!" Lana said, speaking for the first time. "Do you know where he is?"

Now the expression on Katy's face was one of sadness. "Have you not heard? He is dead. He and all the Americans who were with him."

"We heard," Lana said. "But we hoped that it wasn't true."

"I wish I could tell you that it isn't true, but I'm afraid it is," Katy said. "Where are you going, Bob Garrett? Are you looking for Camp Bolivar?"

"Camp Bolivar?"

"It is the camp of the rebels who are fighting against Mendoza."

"Yes, that is what we are looking for. Do you know where it is?"

"Get into the car," Katy said. "I'll take you there."

After a couple of miles, a man in a camouflage uniform suddenly stepped out from behind some shrubbery. Katy stopped and put her window down.

"Emile," she said, smiling at him.

Emile nodded, then looked at Bob and Lana.

"*Quienes son ellos?*" he asked, nodding toward the two Americans.

"Who are they? They are Bob Garrett and Lana Henry," Katy replied. "They are friends of John Barrone and the Americans who helped us."

"I am sorry about your friends," Emile said. He made a motion with his hand. "You may go ahead."

Katy drove another half mile, passing at least three more guards, then parked the car in the middle of what appeared to be a small village.

"I will introduce you to Ricardo Cortina," Katy said as they got out of the car.

They found Ricardo sitting at a table in the dining hall. He was having a cup of coffee and looking over a map. Katy introduced them.

"My nephew, Esteban, is not here right now. He has gone out on a perimeter patrol," Ricardo said. "But I'm sure he would like to meet you as soon as he gets back in."

"Perhaps we will meet him soon," Bob said.

"Are you are going to stay with us?" Ricardo asked.

"Yes. That is, if you will allow us to stay. We are part of the same team and we plan to finish the job our friends started."

"But there were seven of them. There are only two of you."

"I will work four times harder and she will work three times harder. That way we'll be able to make up the difference," Bob said.

For just a moment, Ricardo was confused by the strange reply, then, suddenly he laughed.

"I understand," he said. "It is a good joke."

"Senor Cortina, I am told there were no bodies found."

"That is true."

"Are you convinced . . . totally convinced that they are dead?"

Ricardo sighed. "One always has hope," he replied.

Senate Foreign Relations Committee Hearing Room, Russell Senate Office Building, Washington, D.C.

Harley Thomas sat at a table in the committee hearing room, facing a barrage of United States Senators. Since the testimony would be covering top-secret information, the hearing was closed to the press and public. In fact, nobody but the very insiders even knew that the hearing was taking place.

Senator Avery Chambers, senior senator from Alabama, was the committee chairman. The white-haired senator tapped into the microphone.

Tap, tap, tap.

"Can everybody hear me?" he asked.

Tap, tap, tap.

He blew into it. *Shhhh, shhhh.*

"We can hear you, Senator," someone sitting at the far end of the table responded.

"We've called this hearing at the behest of the senator from the state of Massachusetts, Senator Josh

Kelly. The purpose of this hearing is to delve into the unauthorized and inappropriate participation into the domestic affairs of a foreign, sovereign nation. Would the witness please state his name and position, for the record?"

Harley leaned into the mike. "My name is Harley Marion Thomas. I am director of operations for the Central Intelligence Agency."

"And how long have you been with the CIA?"

"Seventeen years, Senator."

"Thank you. Chair recognizes Senator Kelly."

Kelly leaned forward as if going in for the kill. "Mr. Thomas," he started. "Have you ever heard of a group of illegal mercenaries who call themselves the Code Name Team?"

"No, sir," Thomas said.

"What?" Kelly responded in surprise. "Mr. Thomas, may I remind you that you are under oath? Now, I ask you again, have you ever heard of the Code Name Team?"

"Yes."

It was almost as if Kelly hadn't wanted to hear that answer, because he was all charged up for the kill.

"Then . . . then you admit that you have heard of them?"

"Yes, sir."

"Then why did you say no when I asked you earlier?"

"You didn't ask me earlier."

"Could I have my question read back, please?" Kelly asked impatiently.

"Have you ever heard of a group of illegal mercenaries who call themselves the Code Name Team?" the committee clerk read, tonelessly.

"You asked two different questions, Senator. Your first question was if I had ever heard of a group of *illegal mercenaries* calling themselves the Code Name Team. If there is such a group of *illegal mercenaries* passing themselves off as the Code Name Team, then I am not aware of them. I have, however, heard of the Code Name Team."

A few of the more conservative senators on the committee chuckled.

"All right, all right," Kelly said with a dismissive wave of his hand. "We'll continue. Were you aware that the Code Name Team was conducting clandestine operations in Colombia?"

"I was aware, yes."

"Was the Code Name Team a black ops, authorized by the CIA?"

"It was not."

"Mr. Thomas, I remind you again that you are under oath."

"You don't have to remind me that I am under oath, Senator. I consider myself to be a man of honor, and I take my oath very seriously."

"Then I ask you again. Was the Code Name Team a black operation, funded by and authorized by the CIA? And were you, specifically, the one who authorized them?"

"They were not, and I did not."

In exasperation, Kelly turned to Senator Chambers. "Senator, I will have a witness later whose testimony will directly contradict the testimony of this witness. I believe he is lying, and I want it to go on record, right now, that if we prove he is lying, he will be charged with perjury."

"Very well, Senator Kelly. Senator Moore, you may question the witness."

Moore was a conservative senator from Missouri.

"Mr. Thomas, you said that you were aware that the Code Name Team was operating in Colombia.

Everyone is aware of that now, due to all the recent press regarding the fact that they were all killed. My question for you, sir, is, did you know they were in Colombia before the rest of the nation learned of their participation?"

"Yes, I knew before anyone else knew."

"How did you know?"

"John Barrone, the field leader of the team, was a friend of mine and a former partner in the CIA."

"Did he tell you he was taking a team to Colombia?"

"He did."

"And what was the purpose?"

"Their purpose was to assist a group of Colombian loyalists who are opposed to the secession of Pangea."

"Are you telling this committee that you knew John Barrone was going before he actually went?"

"Yes, that is what I'm telling this committee."

"Did you attempt to dissuade him from going?"

"I did not."

"Did you offer any assistance, privately or government sponsored?"

"I did not."

"Did you offer official, or even unofficial, recognition of his clandestine activity?"

"I did not. In fact, I specifically told him he would not have any CIA support."

"I see. According to the latest news reports, John Barrone and all his team were killed. Do you believe that to be true?"

"I don't know. It could be true, though I pray that it is not."

"What happened, do you know?"

"Senator Kelly came to Langley for a secret meeting with Agent Mark Roberts of the CIA. The purpose of the meeting was to find some way to stop the Code

Name Team, and to provide American assistance to Luiz Mendoza's secession movement."

"Wait a minute, provide American assistance to the secession? I thought we were against that."

"We are, Senator," Agent Thomas replied.

"Go ahead, what else did they discuss?"

"Agent Mark Roberts suggested to Senator Kelly that if he would request Roberts to look into the situation, Roberts could use that ruse to would make the situation ago away.

"Roberts then contacted the Ninth Fusilier Battalion, and Lucas Tyreen, the DEA agent in the field, informing him that the Code Name Team was in Colombia to start their own drug cartel. Roberts suggested that the Code Name Team should be eliminated, with extreme prejudice."

"That means they should be killed," Thomas said.

"So you are saying that the CIA was behind this?"

"No, sir," Thomas said. "The CIA was merely the instrument. The people behind this were Agent Mark Roberts and Senator Josh Kelly."

"What?" Senator Kelly shouted. "Now just wait a minute here! Point of order!"

"Hold on there, Senator, you'll get your chance to respond to this," Senator Chambers said. "Go ahead, Senator Moore, you may continue your questioning."

"Thank you, Senator," Senator Moore said. Then to his witness, "Is there a reason why the Ninth Fusilier Battalion was the one to be contacted?"

"Yes. The Ninth is composed entirely of men from the local area. Although it is currently a member of the Colombian Army, it will be turned over to the Pangean Army as soon as the new country is formed."

"Was there any proof that this Code Name Team was trying to start a drug cartel?" Senator Moore asked.

"No, sir, no proof at all. There had never even been any speculation until Mark Roberts and Senator Kelly raised the issue."

"Mr. Chairman, point of order," Kelly shouted again. "I demand that Mr. Mark Roberts be put on the stand to dispute this . . . this pack of lies."

"Mr. Chairman, I'm sorry, but Mark Roberts won't be able to testify," Harley said.

"And why is that, Mr. Thomas?"

"Mark Roberts committed suicide last night," Harley said.

There were a few gasps from among the senators present.

"Well then, you have no way of proving your contention, do you, Mr. Thomas?" Senator Kelly said, triumphantly.

"Actually, Senator, I do," Harley said. "Before Mark Roberts shot himself, he wrote a long letter, explaining everything that happened and his reasons for participating. The chairman has that letter."

"That letter proves nothing," Kelly said. "Why, it could be forged."

"No," Harley said. "Say what you may about Mark Roberts, he had been in the agency for a long time and he knew bureaucracy. He had the letter notarized."

Chapter 20

Remote area of the jungle

They had been trekking through the jungle for nearly a week now. The going was hard and slow because they had evacuated the house so quickly that they took nothing with them, other than the weapons they had on their person, and the packets of money they had managed to liberate from the millions, just before Jennifer burned it.

They counted their money on the first night and discovered that they had a little over a quarter of a million dollars. Nothing like the bankroll they had just before the attack, but, under the circumstances, a significant amount.

Their biggest problem during the trek through the jungle was food. While lamenting over the fact that they had five hundred MREs back in camp, they were limited for the first two days to eating grasshoppers and grub worms. On the third day they saw a small, feral pig and shot it. They cooked it over an open fire and, even though they had no seasoning of any kind, it was a feast compared to what they had been through.

Part of what slowed them down was the fact that they were taking Mike's body with them. Just before the final collapse of the house, John had pushed

Mike's body over the edge of the cliff. It wasn't something he wanted to do, but as Mike was already dead, the fall wasn't going to hurt him, and John didn't want to let him burn up in the fire.

By the fourth day, though, they were beginning to have second thoughts about carrying him. It was hot in the jungle and decomposition was setting in, making it very, very difficult to carry him. They were wondering what to do with him, when Paul happened to see a small cabin.

"Is it occupied?" John asked.

"Yes."

"Let's pay them a visit," John suggested.

Paul started to go with John, but John held up his hand to stop him. "I think it would be better if I took one of the women with me," he said. "A man and a woman will cause less concern than two men."

"How are you going to explain showing up in the middle of the jungle?" Chris asked.

"Airplane crash?" Linda suggested.

John nodded. "Good idea," he said.

"See if they've got any food," Don said.

"Come along, Linda," John said. "Since the airplane crash was your idea, you can help me pull it off."

Leaving the others behind, John and Linda approached the little house. They didn't have to pretend to be bedraggled, they looked it because they were. A woman was on the back porch of the house, washing clothes in a big tub.

"Please, can you help us? We need help," John called out in English, then repeated it in Spanish. "*Por favor, necesitamos la ayuda.*"

The woman gasped and put her hand to her mouth in fright.

"Don't be frightened," John said. "We are Americans. Our airplane crashed in the jungle."

When it was obvious that the woman didn't understand English, he said it again in Spanish.

Once she was convinced that they meant her no harm, the woman was less frightened and asked what she could do to help.

"You could go for help," he said in Spanish. He took out two one-hundred-dollar bills. "This is half a million pesos," he said. "*Medio millón de pesos.*"

The woman's eyes grew wide in awe, and she took the money.

"It's yours," John said, "if you will go get help for us."

"*Sí,*" the woman said, nodding.

"How far must you go?"

"*Cinco kilómetros en aquella dirección,*" she said.

"Five clicks that way," John said to Linda. So, that's about six miles round-trip. It ought to give us enough time."

"Enough time to do what?"

"Enough time to get something to eat and bury Mike," he said.

> *TO WHOEVER FINDS THIS BODY:*
> *It is our hope that nobody finds this body, because we plan to return and take it back to the United States for a burial with the honor and distinction this noble soul deserves.*
> *The fact that you have discovered this body means that, for some reason, we were unable to return. Therefore, we want you to know who this is, and pray that you will take a moment to honor him.*
> *His name is Michel Jorge Rojas. His friends called him Mike. Mike was of Mexican descent, but he was one hundred percent American and was proud of the fact that one of his ancestors had been at the Alamo, FIGHTING ON THE SIDE OF THE TEXANS.*

While carrying on the proud tradition of honor started by his ancestor so many years ago, Mike was killed in the line of duty. He was a close and loyal friend to those whose names are hereto attached, and we will miss him.

s/John Barrone, Chris Farmer, Paul Brewer, Don Yee, Linda Marsh, Jennifer Barnes.

Once the note was finished and signed by all, John sealed it up in a jar, then laid the jar on top of the waterproof bag in which Mike's body had been placed. Then, Chris and Paul lowered him into the grave they had dug. Once he was in the hole, Chris and Paul began closing the grave.

"Don, have you figured out how to find this place again?" John asked.

"It's not going to be that easy without a GPS to mark the position," Don said.

"Use your brains. You're supposed to be a mathematical wizard, aren't you?"

"That just means my fingers fly on a keyboard," Don replied. "Do you see any keyboards handy?"

"You can do it, I know you can," John said. "You didn't think you could climb down the cliff behind the house, but you got down, didn't you?"

"I got down all right, but I didn't climb."

"Then how did you do it?"

"I don't know, but I think I levitated," Don said.

The men were burying Mike in the backyard of the house. The waterproof tarp in which the body was wrapped, the paper on which the note was written, and the jar in which it was placed, had all come from a search of the house, empty now that the woman was gone.

In conversation with the woman, just before she left, they learned that her husband worked on a coffee plantation, staying there during the week and coming home only on weekends. That meant they had little danger of being discovered while she was gone.

While the men worked in the backyard, Linda and Jennifer found enough food in the house to prepare a meal of rice and beans for all of them. They ate the meal, then left another two hundred dollars on the table for her.

"Let's go," John said. "We want to be out of here before she comes back, and we have a long hike back to Camp Bolivar."

Camp Bolivar

Bob and Lana were in the dining hall talking to Ricardo when Palo came in with a big smile on his face.

"Don Ricardo, they are here," he said, speaking in English.

"What? Who is here?"

"Our American friends," Palo said. "They are not dead! They are here, coming into the camp now!"

"Oh!" Lana said. "Oh, are you sure?"

"*Sí*, I am sure," Palo said. "You can look for yourselves, they are in the village."

Bob and Lana got up and hurried to the door. Looking outside, they saw a group of happy people crowding around a smaller group.

"It is them, Lana," Bob said excitedly.

Bob and Lana left the dining hall and walked quickly toward their friends, but because so many well-wishers were crowded around them, neither John nor any of the others of the Code Name Team saw the two approach.

Bob pushed his way gently through the crowd and

stood right in front of John. The expression of surprise on John's face made it all worthwhile.

Bob extended his hand.

"Dr. Livingstone, I presume?" he said.

"At your service, Mr. Stanley," John replied.

What followed were warm and heartfelt greetings between the old friends. It was Lana who noticed the absence.

"Mike?" she said.

The happy smiles fell away, and John shook his head, slowly.

"Mike didn't make it," he said.

Tears began to slide down Lana's cheeks, and Linda stepped toward her to embrace her. Linda had already been through her grieving, so she knew what Lana was going through.

"Ricardo, is there anything to eat around here?" Don asked.

"Why don't you all go into the dining room and I'll have the cook prepare something for you?" Ricardo replied.

"Good. And maybe some sort of sandwich to tide me over until dinner is cooked?"

"I'm sure we can find something," Ricardo promised.

The Code Name Team went into the dining hall where they all sat around one long table, enjoying their reunion. Then, almost as an afterthought, Bob pulled out his satellite phone. "I need to report in to Wagner," he said.

"Yeah, do that," Chris quipped. "Otherwise the son of a bitch will be going through all our things, taking the good stuff for himself."

Bob got Wagner on the phone.

"I have made contact," he said.

"What have you found out?" Wagner asked anxiously.

"The news is mixed," Bob reported. "I am sorry to say that Mike is dead, but the others are here, and they are fine."

There was a beat of silence from Wagner's end, then he said, "You're right, the news is mixed. It's very sad about Mike, but I'm glad to hear that we didn't lose them all."

"What's next for Lana and me?" Bob asked.

"It's John's call," Wagner said. "Since you are already there, if he wants to use you, he can. We have nothing going on back here."

Bob looked over at John. "John, can you find a place for Lana and me?"

"Absolutely," John replied.

Bob went back to the phone. "We're going to stay."

"All right, be careful, and good luck to you."

After Bob hung up, he, Lana, and the others visited for several minutes, catching each other up on events. John told about being set up and ambushed for their first mission, then being attacked in their safe house. "I don't know who it was that attacked us," he said. "But they were certainly well equipped. It almost had to be Mendoza."

Bob shook his head. "The news reports back home said that it was the Colombian Army."

"Colombian Army? Why would they attack us?"

"According to Senator Kelly, it's because you were trying to set up your own drug cartel down here."

"Damn. How the hell did Kelly get involved in this?"

"He's hitting all the talking-head shows back home, telling everyone how we should recognize Pangea."

"He's full of shit," John said. "By the way, how did you manage to find us?"

"We didn't find you. We found this camp and you showed up."

"I mean how did you find the camp?"

Bob told about their encounter with Viktor Marin.

"He brought us as far as the suspension bridge, then he went back," Bob said.

"No doubt to report to Mendoza what he had done."

"You think Marin is in Mendoza's camp?"

"Of course he is in Mendoza's camp. Marin is a whore, who will sell his charms to anyone who pays him."

"Oh, damn," Chris said. "Marin is a whore selling his charms? Couldn't you have come up with a better analogy than that?"

The others laughed.

At that moment, Ricardo Cortina came back into the dining hall, accompanied this time by his nephew. Esteban was wearing camouflage fatigues and carrying a rifle, indicative of having just come back from patrol.

"Look who just arrived from Cali," Ricardo said.

"John, you are safe!" Esteban said with a big smile. He hurried across the room to embrace John and the others. "Oh, I was so certain you were all dead! It's in all the newspapers."

"So we heard," John replied.

As Esteban went around greeting all of them, the smile on his face disappeared when he noticed that one was missing.

"Rojas?" he asked.

Chris shook his head. "He didn't make it. He was killed when the house was attacked."

"Oh, I am terribly sorry."

"Esteban, Bob says the report is that we were attacked by the Colombian Army. Is that right?"

"Yes," Esteban said.

"But why would they attack us? We're on their side."

"The Ninth Fusiliers is part of the Colombian Army, but Mendoza controls them."

"What I want to know is, how did they know we were there? That was supposed to be our safe house."

"Oh," Esteban said. "I almost forgot. One of the reasons I came out here today was to give you warning."

"Warning?" Ricardo asked. "Warning about what?"

"Uncle, Gustavo De Soto came in. He is the son of Manuel De Soto, the man who furnished the safe house."

"Yes, yes, I know who Manuel De Soto is. And his son. So he has joined us, eh? Good, good."

"More than that, Uncle," Esteban said. "Thanks to him, I now know who has been betraying us."

"Oh?"

"It is Katy Correal," Esteban said.

"What? Katy Correal? Are you certain of this, Nephew?"

"*Sí*, I am certain. She was seen going into Mendoza's house the other night, and she didn't come out until the next morning."

"Damn," Bob said. "She's the one who picked Lana and me up after we crossed the bridge."

"You mean Katy is in camp?" Esteban asked.

"*Sí*, she is in camp," Ricardo said. "She came in while you were on patrol."

"Uncle, we must stop her before she does more damage."

"Stop her? Stop her how?" Ricardo asked.

"There is only one way to stop her, Uncle. And you know what it is."

"No," Ricardo said, shaking his head. "I will see to it that she can't do us any more harm, but I will not kill her."

"John, my friend, I apologize to you for what happened to you and to Michel," Esteban said.

"That's all right, it wasn't your fault," John said. "These things happen. At least, we found out about it before she could do us any further harm."

Chapter 21

Camp Bolivar

It was early morning and the camp smelled of frying bacon, baking bread, and steaming coffee. The Code Name Team was outside the billets, sitting on boxes, stumps, logs, whatever they could find.

"I hate that about Katy," Bob said. "She seemed so nice."

"You mean she seemed so pretty," Lana said.

"No, that's not it."

"Ha! My ass, that's not it. She had you salivating over her like an eighteen-year-old boy with a college cheerleader."

"Watch that kind of talk," Paul said. "You're getting too close to Don's fantasies now."

The others laughed.

"Well, all you have to do is think of Brian Skipper," John said. "She had his number, and look where it got him."

"I thought for a while there that she had your number as well," Don said.

"No," Jennifer said. "I can tell you for a fact that she didn't."

"I wonder why she did it," Linda said.

"Esteban said she was sleeping with Mendoza. I

guess being the first lady . . . or even the first whore . . . has its compensations."

"How much longer until breakfast?" Don asked. "I'm hungry."

"Now, there's a revelation," John said sarcastically. "Don's hungry."

Chris heard it first, calling it up from some deep, recessed memory of his days in the Gulf War. It sounded rather like an empty freight car rolling down a railroad track.

"Incoming!" he shouted, diving for the ground.

None of the others actually recognized the sound, since none of them had ever been exposed to it, but they knew how to react first and ask questions later, so they dived to the ground as soon as Chris did.

The arcing sound continued for another few seconds, then there was an explosion in one of the small, family quarters.

Almost right on top of that, came several more arcing sounds, followed quickly by explosions.

"Son of a bitch! They're using artillery on us!" Chris said.

The next thing they heard was the low growl of helicopter engines. They could hear them, but not see them. Then, popping up just over the tree line, were two Bell Jet Rangers. They were firing rockets into the camp, and as people ran across the camp parade ground, they were cut down by machine-gun fire from the helicopters.

When the helicopters pulled up from their firing run, John got a good look at them. They were painted olive drab, and on the tail cone was a white ball inside an orange circle. Inside the white ball was a black, four-corner star.

"Damn!" Paul said. "That's the symbol of Pangea! They've got their own air force now?"

"We've got to get these people organized," John said. "I'm pretty damn sure this isn't all they have in mind for us. Chris, you bring my weapon!"

"Right!" Chris said.

As the rest of the team started after the weapons, John ran to the steel ring and began clanging it loudly. To his relief, the training exercises had paid off, because he saw women and children running toward the bunkers.

To his horror, one woman and three children didn't make it. A shell landed right on top of them, and when the smoke of the explosion cleared away, there was nothing left but a jumbled pile of bloody clothes and body parts.

Another building went up as the helicopters came back across, firing a second barrage of rockets.

John saw Palo.

"Palo, find Esteban," John said. "Get your men armed and in position to resist the attack! Make certain you bring enough ammunition with you!"

"I haven't seen Esteban," Palo said. "He may have been hit!"

"Who is his second in command?"

"Juan Bustamante."

"Tell Bustamante he is in charge until Esteban shows up."

"Right," Palo said.

It took less than a minute for the entire Code Name Team to return to the billets, all of them armed.

"Get to the berm," John said.

"Right," Chris replied, and the team ran to the berm to help with the defense.

"John! John! Please! Let me out of here!"

John recognized Katy's voice and saw her looking out through a small window in the back of the head-quarters building. This was the storeroom, and the only room in the entire compound that could be locked from the outside, so it stood to reason that's where she had been put. John walked back to the window.

"Please, let me out of here!" Katy called. "I'm frightened!"

"Yeah? Well, you should have thought about that when you told Mendoza where we were. You figured you would be out of here by now, didn't you?"

"What? I didn't tell Mendoza where we were."

Another shell came in, bursting in the building next door. John could feel a blast of heat and the stinging residue of splinters, but he wasn't hurt.

"John, please, I'll be killed."

John started to leave her, figuring it would be good enough for her, but he couldn't bring himself to do it.

"All right," he said. "Hang on, I'll get you out."

As he ran back to the front of the building, one of the helicopters made another pass, but this time every weapon in the camp was firing at it. John saw the helicopter pitch forward, then plunge down into the jungle, followed almost immediately by a ball of fire and a plume of smoke. The heavy thump of the explosion reached his ears a couple of seconds later. The camp cheered.

John went in through the front door of the headquarters building, then hurried to the back. The door to the storeroom was held shut with a padlock. Not taking the time to look for a key, John shouted out, "Stay back from the door, I'm going to shoot the lock off."

John fired one shot from his Glock pistol, and the bullet cut through the hasp. He pulled it off and jerked the door open.

"Come on," he said.

"Oh, thank you," Katy said in relief.

Just before they started to the front, a shell hit the building, bringing it crashing down around them.

John went down under the collapsing ceiling, but a sturdy table prevented him for being hurt.

"Are you okay?" he shouted.

"Yes," she answered, coughing in the dust. Like John, she had instinctively dived under the table and, like him, was spared any serious injury. "How are we going to get out of here?"

"We're going to dig our way out," John said.

"John, I'm not your spy," Katy said. "Please believe me."

"Yeah, well, Brian Skipper believed you, and look what happened to him," John said.

"I didn't have anything to do with Brian's death," Katy replied.

"I suppose you're going to tell me you loved him."

"No," Katy said. "I liked him, and I led him to believe that I loved him. But he was an assignment."

"An assignment?"

"Yes."

"And what about Mendoza? Was sleeping with him an assignment also?"

"Yes."

"You are too much, woman, do you know that? You feed me a line of bullshit and expect me to believe it? You are just too damn much."

"John, I am a deep-cover agent with the Ministry of Justice."

"Right, and I'm a world-champion fandango dancer," John replied sarcastically.

"I'm telling the truth. Not everyone in the Colombian Government is in favor of splitting our country asunder. My job was to stop Mendoza by whatever means it takes."

"I see, and you thought sleeping with him would do it?"

"By whatever means it takes," Katy said again.

"And did that include setting us up at Jungle Camp One? Did that include telling Mendoza where our safe house was?"

"I didn't do that."

"It had to be you," John replied. "You are the only one who knew about the attack on the drug factory and the location of the safe house."

"Esteban also knew."

"You forget, Esteban was with us on the mission to the drug factory. He could have been killed. Besides, he's Ricardo's nephew. He's a blood relative."

"As I understand it, he chose to approach from the south, did he not?"

"What does that have to do with it?"

"I understand that the Claymores were all pointing north. He wasn't in as much danger as it appeared. Besides, he's not a blood relative," Katy said.

"What do you mean he's not a blood relative?"

"Ricardo's brother married Esteban's mother, then adopted Esteban. Before he was Esteban Cortina, he was Esteban Penstraza. And his mother's maiden name was Mendoza."

All the time they were talking, John had been kicking pieces of timber aside. He turned toward Katy when she said that.

"What?"

"Esteban's mother was Mendoza's sister."

"Are you lying to me?"

"It's easy enough to check out," Katy said.

Pulling aside one more large piece of timber, John was rewarded by seeing the light of day. Then, leaning over to look at it, he saw that it was a big enough opening to allow them through.

"Normally, I would say ladies first," John said. "But I don't intend to let you get away from me, so I'm going out first."

John wriggled through, then waited for Katy. He helped her through.

"Let's get out of here," he said.

Leaving the collapsed building, they ran across the parade ground until they reached the berm, then went over the top.

"You made it," Chris said. "I was beginning to worry."

"Everybody in place?" John asked.

"Yes, let the bastards come," Chris said. "We're ready for them."

"That's good," Paul shouted. "Because here they come!"

Looking back toward the west end, or open end, of the camp, John saw several dozen skirmishers advancing toward them.

"Hold your fire until they reach the flagpole," he shouted. "*No dispare hasta que el enemigo alcance el poste de bandera!*" he repeated in Spanish.

The order was repeated up and down the line as determined men sighted down the barrels of their weapons, holding fire as directed, watching as the army came toward them.

The enemy continued to advance, firing as they did so. When the lead element reached the flagpole, John shouted, "Now!"

Every weapon behind the berm opened up, including the two M-60 machine guns. The fire was devastating and the advancing soldiers were cut down like wheat. Those who weren't cut down retreated from the field.

After a few more minutes, the soldiers began dropping mortar rounds in behind the berm. This was effective and it created several casualties among the defenders.

The mortar rounds stopped, and after a few minutes, another wave of attackers approached. This time they were a little smarter. Rather than advancing up through the middle of the parade ground as they had the first time, they moved in as skirmishers, using the individual houses to shield their approach.

Because they had the cover and concealment of the houses, they weren't driven away the way they were the first time, and it turned into a fixed gun battle with each side taking casualties.

Ricardo came running down the line, bent over at the waist to take advantage of the berm. He stopped in surprise when he saw Katy sitting quietly at the foot of the berm. "What is she doing here?"

"I couldn't leave her locked up in the storeroom, she might have been killed."

Ricardo sighed, then nodded. "Yes," he said. "You did the right thing by letting her out. As long as she is in our custody, we are responsible for her safety."

"I'm glad you feel that way, because I'm going to leave you in charge of her," John said.

"All right. I'll take her into the command bunker," Ricardo said.

"Ricardo, ask Palo and Esteban to come see me," John said. "We have to come up with some way to break this standoff."

"Esteban is not here," Ricardo answered.

"What? You mean he still hasn't shown up?"

"No, and I'm worried about him. He went out on another patrol late last night, and he hasn't come back. I fear he may have been captured."

John looked toward Katy, but she registered no reaction to the news.

"There's always the chance that he just got caught out there and can't get back in," John suggested.

"Yes," Ricardo said. "There is also that chance."

John put his arm on Ricardo's shoulder. "I'm worried about him too," he said. "Even though he isn't blood kin to me the way he is to you."

Ricardo shook his head. "He's not my blood kin. My brother adopted him when he was a young boy."

Again, John looked at Katy, and again, she showed no response. He decided he would not like to play poker with this woman.

"Well, adopted or not, he is your nephew, and I know how worried you must feel. But right now we are in the midst of a war, so we need to get organized and stay focused. What is our casualty count?"

"Seven killed, ten wounded. But only one wound is severe."

"How severe?"

Ricardo shook his head. "He won't make it through the day."

"Too bad," John said.

"John," Jennifer called. "Nearly all of them have pulled back out."

"Yeah," John said. "They may be regrouping for something else."

They waited for half an hour, but nothing happened.

"What are they trying to do, wait us out?" Bob asked.

"I guess they figure that the longer they wait, the more nervous we will be," John said.

They waited for another fifteen minutes, then John called to Chris.

"Chris, grab your sniper rifle and come with me. Let's see if we can make something happen. I'll be your spotter."

"Right," Chris said.

"You two be careful," Linda called out. "We've lost Mike, I wouldn't want to lose anyone else."

John and Chris left the camp by the south end, climbing up the rope ladder on the side of the cliff.

As soon as they reached the top, they started east, running just behind the crest so they couldn't be seen against the sky. Less than a half mile east of the camp, they saw the army that was poised to attack them.

"All right," John said. "Pick out a good position and let's get busy."

Chris nodded, then found a spot that would allow him an unrestricted field of fire at whatever targets John selected. John raised his binoculars and started searching through the assembled men, looking for the best target.

"Damn, Ricardo was right," he said.

"Right about what?"

"They've got Esteban. They've taken him prisoner."

John continued to study Esteban through his glasses. Esteban was just standing there, with his arms behind his back.

One of the officers approached Esteban, carrying what might have been a map. He pointed to the map and asked Esteban something.

"Spit in his face, Esteban," John said under his breath as he continued to monitor Esteban's situation.

Then, to John's surprise, Esteban brought his arms around front. But how could that be unless . . . "What the hell! He's not handcuffed," John said aloud.

Esteban pointed to something on the map, then to the two mountain ranges that flanked the camp.

"Well, I'll be damned," John said. "Katy was right. The son of a bitch is helping the other side."

"If he is a prisoner, he may be helping them under coercion," Chris suggested.

As John continued to stare at Esteban, he saw Esteban call out to a passing soldier. The soldier stopped and saluted, and Esteban saluted back. It wasn't until then that John noticed Esteban was wearing shoulder epaulets. On his epaulets were three stars, with a bar across the center star. He was wearing the rank of a full colonel.

"I take that back," John said. "He isn't just working with them . . . he *is* them."

"Want me to take him down?" Chris asked.

"Yes," John said. "Hit the son of a bitch." Quickly, he corrected himself. "No, wait. I am going to have you take him down, but let's see if we can pick out about five more of their officers. We may well have the opportunity to stop this thing here and now."

John took the next few minutes, seeking out the highest-ranking officers he could find. He located a lieutenant colonel, two stars and a bar, a major, one star and a bar, and two captains, each of whom was wearing the three stars indicative of their rank.

"All right," John said. "I've got them located. Take out Esteban first."

Chris squeezed the trigger and John saw Esteban grab his throat, just before he dropped.

Working quickly, Chris fired four more times, taking out the next four ranking officers.

Chris's one-man attack turned out to be very successful. When they saw their officers go down around them, dropping like flies from an unseen sniper, the soldiers were thrown into a panic.

Some of them started running then, and their running spread throughout the ranks until the entire army was streaming back into the jungle. Within moments more than three-fourths of the attacking army had abandoned the field, and those who were left were milling around in total confusion. Then, finally, they too left the field, though in somewhat less of a panic than those who had fled before them.

Buenaventura, Colombia, Mendoza's estate

Mendoza slammed the telephone down in disgust. "The bastards lied to me, Gato!" he said, angrily. "Congress is not going to vote for the independence of Pangea."

Mendoza did not get an answer.

"Gato? Gato, where are you?"

Mendoza started through the house, looking for Gato, but to no avail. It wasn't until then that he noticed he was alone in the house. Not only had Gato deserted him, but so had all of the servants. He picked up the phone and called the guard gate.

There was no answer.

"What the hell?" he said aloud. "Has everyone deserted me?"

Mendoza poured himself a large glass of whiskey, tossed it down, then picked up the bottle. He was about to pour himself another drink, but decided not to. Instead, he took the bottle over to a large blue leather chair and sat down. Picking up the remote, he turned on the TV.

The scene on the screen was of several thousand people crowding the streets of various Colombian cities.

"The scene was the same in Bogata, Cali, and Medellin," the announcer was saying. "All Colombians are celebrating the fact that the nation is not going to be split into two countries."

Mendoza was halfway through his third glass of

whiskey, morbidly watching the street celebrations of his defeat, when he became aware of a subtle fragrance: sandalwood and vetiver, with a floral touch, and musky undertones. When he looked around, he saw that he wasn't alone.

He smiled and stood up.

"I knew you wouldn't desert me. Everyone else has, but I knew you wouldn't."

Mendoza's only answer was the subdued snap of three shots, fired from a silencer-equipped pistol. All three shots hit him in the heart and he dropped his drink, then fell back into his chair.

Code Name Headquarters, southwest Texas

"What time is the ceremony?" Paul asked as he pulled the collar away from his neck.

"Fourteen hundred," Bob replied. Like Paul, and every other member of the Code Name Team, including Wagner, Bob was wearing a suit and tie. They were gathered in the den of the headquarters house, waiting for the ceremony to begin.

The large-screen TV was on and a newscast was going, playing to an inattentive crowd.

"It's a bull market so far today, with brisk trading sending the Dow up by 119 points. S and P is up by fifteen."

Suddenly the routine news was interrupted by an alert, and the music that signaled the alert caught everyone's attention.

"This just in. Our news bureau in Washington has learned that Senator Josh Kelly, longtime fixture in the U.S. Senate, and often mentioned as a possible presidential candidate, is planning to give up his seat, effective immediately.

"Senator Kelly lost a tremendous amount of political capital and prestige when he backed the late Luiz Mendoza in his bid to take a rather large section of land away from Colombia and create the new nation of Pangea.

"Bitter fighting broke out between those loyal to the Colombian Government and those who favored secession. Ironically in the biggest battle, the rebels represented the government of Colombia, while the Ninth Fusiliers, ostensibly a part of the Colombian Army, had already defected to the Pangeans.

"Mendoza was found dead in his palatial residence, shortly after that battle concluded. The cause of death has been listed as suicide, though as he was shot three times, some are questioning the official findings."

"Turn it off," John said. "If everyone is ready, I think it's about time to go pay respects to our brother."

A lone grave, behind the Code Name Headquarters

A single white cross stood over a little pile of freshly turned dirt. No one was present except for the Code Name Team, and they stood in silent rows along each side of the grave. The inscription on the cross read:

Michel Jorges Rojas
A Proud American

"Lord," John said, "there's no need for me to say much. Mike's family is here, and we knew him, and we know how blessed we were to have known him.

"You knew him too, I reckon," he continued. "So I don't need to be telling you anything about him. I just hope you understand that you are getting one of the very best."

John looked at the others, at the long, sad faces of the men, and the tearstained cheeks of the women.

"Ladies and gentlemen, arm yourselves for the rendering of honors."

All the members of the Code Name Team reached down beside them.

"Present arms!"

As if on parade, the nine bent their arms at the elbow, thrusting beer cans out in front of them.

"Prepare arms!"

Again, in perfect synchronization, the pull tabs were jerked from the top of the cans.

"Ready!"

The beer cans were thrust forward, over Mike's grave.

"Aim!"

The cans were tilted forty-five degrees.

"Fire!"

All nine cans were inverted over the grave, and nine streams of amber liquid cascaded down onto the dirt. Then, rather than pool on the dirt as they expected it to do, the beer leached down through the topsoil.

"Wow! Look at Mike suck that beer up!" Chris said.

Despite the solemnity of the occasion, the others laughed.

Then, as had been prearranged, everyone left the graveside but Lana. This was to allow her a few private words with Mike. Lana was followed by Jennifer, then Linda, then the men, one by one until it came to John. John was the last one to speak.

"Mike, I want you to look up Michelle. You'll like her, and she'll like you. Also, she's been there longer than you, so, if you'll let her, she can kind of look after you . . . make things easier for you.

"Listen, I've never figured out whether or not you folks can look down on us from there, but if you can, I promise never to do anything that will make you ashamed of the fact that you were a member of the Code Name Team.

"*Vaya con Dios,* my friend. I'll see you around."

Leaving the grave site, John joined the others, and they walked back into the house. In the southwest sky, lightning flashed and there was a long, low rumble of rolling thunder.

"Did you hear that?" John asked.

"What, you mean the thunder?" Bob replied.

John shook his head. "That wasn't thunder," he said. "That was Mike, telling us good-bye."

Turn the page for an exciting preview of

VENGEANCE IS MINE

The new thriller from William W. Johnstone
and Fred Austin

They've already started coming across. The drug dealers
and the petty criminals. The terrorists and the parasites.
For one man on the west Texas border, the time to stand
against them is now. John Howard Stark, a Vietnam vet
whose family has worked their ranch for generations, has
set off a trip wire—and an ambush has exploded all around
him. A Colombian drug cartel commander, with the help of
an ex-special forces hit man and his own deadly army, has
already slaughtered three Americans—including Stark's
uncle and his neighbor—and will slaughter anyone else
who stands in his way. The local law is in his pocket and the
border patrol is powerless to help.

VENGEANCE IS MINE

A timeless story—ripped from today's headlines!

Now John Howard Stark is about to wage a one-man
war. And he's got the best kind of reason to fight to the
death. But for this American, there's one thing more
dangerous than the enemies slithering across the border—
and that's the second enemy standing behind his back:
his own government . . .

VENGEANCE IS MINE

Coming in June 2005

Available wherever Pinnacle Books are sold.

Chapter 1

"Damn it!" John Howard Stark crumpled the newspaper and flung it away from him.

"What is it?" his wife, Elaine, asked from the stove where she was frying bacon. "The Cowboys do something you don't agree with again?"

"Worse'n that. They found another of those damn mad cows up in Washington."

"Oh." Elaine had been a rancher's wife for over thirty years. She knew how something thousands of miles away, like in the Pacific Northwest, could affect life here in the Rio Grande Valley of Texas. Every time there was another outbreak of mad cow disease anywhere in the country, it made beef prices go down, and that hurt ranchers everywhere.

Stark thought the smell of bacon cooking was just about the best smell in the world. He also thought his wife, still slim and straight with only a little gray in her blond hair despite her five-plus decades on earth, was the prettiest sight. But neither of them could cheer him up now. There had been too much bad news for too long. No real catastrophes, mind, just a seemingly endless stream of developments that made things worse and then worse and then worse again. Stark was fed up. Why, for two cents he'd—

He'd do exactly the same things he had done in his life, the rational part of his brain told him. Regrets were worth just about as much as a bucket of warm spit.

Sitting around and moaning wasn't a trait that ran in the Stark family. John Howard's great-great-grandfather had been a frontier judge, a man who had dispensed justice just as easily with a six-gun as with a gavel and a law book. His great-grandfather had worn the badge of county sheriff until settling down to establish this ranch up the Rio Grande from Del Rio. He had faced down some of Pancho Villa's men to keep it. The generations since had hung on to the Diamond S through good times and bad. John Howard himself had left the place for only one extended period of time in his life—to take a trip for Uncle Sam to a backwater country in Southeast Asia where little fellas in black pajamas shot at him for a couple of years. In the more than three decades since then, he had returned to his home, married his high school sweetheart, raised two boys with her, seen both his parents pass away, and taken over the running of the ranch. It was a hardscrabble spread and a hardscrabble time, here in the first decade of the twenty-first century. And Stark wasn't as young as he used to be. Fifty-four years old, by God. He had gone to Vietnam at the ripe old age of eighteen, little more than a boy. But he had returned as a man.

That was a long time ago now. For the first few years, Stark had sometimes woken up in the middle of the night shaking and drenched with sweat. He never could remember the dreams that provoked that reaction in him, but he knew they must have been bad ones. He had seen so many men that the war just wouldn't let go of, so they tried to escape it with drugs and booze and God knows what-all. Ruined past, ruined present, ruined future. He'd been one of the lucky ones. He had Elaine and his folks and the ranch. Later he'd had the boys, David and Peter. They all got him through the nightmare landscape that had claimed so many other men, and these days Stark seldom ever thought about Vietnam. When he did he thought not about the dying but about the friends he had made there.

He'd been too busy lately to think about the past. Like all the other ranchers in Val Verde County, he was struggling to make ends meet. Beef prices were in the crapper, and ever-spiraling taxes and overbearing government regulations didn't help matters, either. Most of the time he felt older than dirt.

But like the old saying went, gettin' old sure as hell beat the alternative. Most of the time Stark figured that was true.

Elaine put a plate full of bacon, biscuits, and scrambled eggs in front of him. The eggs had a lot of peppers and cheese in them, just the way Stark liked them. He poked at them with his fork and said, "This ain't some of that egg substitute stuff, is it?" He would have used a stronger word than "stuff" if not for the fact that Elaine didn't allow any cussing at the kitchen table.

"No, it's the real thing, John Howard," she said. "I've given up on trying to feed you healthy food. You kick up a fuss just like a little baby. Besides, you're going to be just like your daddy and your uncle and your granddaddy and all the other men in your family. You all pack away the red meat and the grease and you're still out reshingling the well house and roping steers when you're ninety-five."

"Yeah, but I don't drink much and only smoke one cigar a year, on my birthday."

She patted him on the shoulder. "I'm sure that's the secret."

She started to turn away, but Stark reached out, lopped an arm around her slender waist, and pulled her onto his lap. Despite her appearance, she wasn't a little bitty thing. She was tall and had some heft to her. But Stark was six-feet-four and weighed two hundred and thirty pounds—only up ten pounds from his fighting weight—and his active life kept him vital and strong in spite of the aches and pains that reminded him of his age. He put his other hand behind Elaine's head and kissed her. She responded with the eagerness that he still aroused in her. In fact, she was a little breathless by the time they broke the kiss.

"That right there, that's the secret," John Howard said.

"What, that all you Stark men are horny old bastards?"

"Damn right."

She laughed and pressed her lips to his again and when she slipped out of his arms he let her go this time. "Eat your breakfast," she said. "We've both got work to do."

Stark nodded as he dug the fork into the eggs and picked up a biscuit. "Yeah, I've got to go over to Tommy's in a little while. One of his cows got over on our range yesterday and bogged down in that sinkhole on the creek. I had to pull her out, and I've got her and her calf out in the barn. I need to find out what he wants to do about them."

"You be sure and tell him hello for me. And remind him that we're expecting him and Julie and the kids over here tomorrow evening."

Stark nodded. He couldn't answer. His mouth was full of bacon and eggs and biscuit by now, and somehow his bad mood of a few minutes earlier had evaporated.

Tomas Carranza—Tommy to his friends—owned the ten thousand acres next to John Howard Stark's Diamond S. It was a small spread for Texas, but Tommy had a small herd. The ranch had belonged to the Carranza family for generations, just as the neighboring land had belonged to the Starks. There had been Carranzas in Sam Houston's army at San Jacinto, fierce *Tejanos* who hated Santa Anna and the oppressive rule of the Mexican dictator every bit as much as the Anglos did. Later the family had settled along the Rio Grande, founding the fine little rancho on the Texas side of the river.

John Howard Stark had always been something of a hero to Tommy Carranza. Tommy was considerably younger. When Tommy was a little boy, Stark was the star of the Del Rio High School baseball team, belting a record number of home runs. Tommy loved baseball, and it was special to have a godlike figure such as John Howard Stark befriend him back then.

But John Howard had graduated and gone off to fight in Vietnam, and Tommy had feared that he would never see his friend again. He had prayed to the Blessed Virgin every night to watch over John Howard, and when Stark came back safely from the war, Tommy felt a secret, never-expressed pride that perhaps his prayers had had something to do with that.

Over the years since, the age difference between the two men, never all that important, had come to matter even less. They regarded each other as equals and good friends. John Howard and Elaine were godparents to the two children Tommy had with his wife, Julie. Hardly a month went by when the families didn't get together for a barbecue. In fact, one of the get-togethers was coming up the next day, the Fourth of July.

On this morning Tommy wasn't thinking about barbecue. He had driven the pickup into Del Rio to get some rolls of fence at the big building supply warehouse store on the edge of town. His land stretched for nearly five miles along the Rio Grande, and Tommy tried to keep every foot of it fenced. The fences kept getting cut, though, by the damned coyotes who trafficked in human cargo and the even more vile drug runners who smuggled their poison across the river.

Sometimes Tommy thought it would be easier just to give up and let the animals take over. But the spirits of his *Tejano* ancestors wouldn't let that happen. A Carranza never gave up the fight.

He wrestled the last roll of wire from the flatbed cart into the back of the pickup and then slammed the tailgate. He rolled the cart to one of the little corral places scattered around the big parking lot, and as he turned back toward his truck he was surprised to see a man standing beside it. The fact that the man stood there was less surprising than the way he looked.

The guy was wearing a suit, for God's sake!

Part of a suit, anyway. He had taken off the jacket and had it draped over one arm. He had also rolled up his sleeves and loosened his tie. The man was stocky, with thinning pale hair. His skin was turning pink in the sun. The suit and the shoes he wore were probably worth more than the battered old pickup beside which he stood.

Tommy thumbed back his straw Stetson with its tightly curled brim and nodded to the stranger. "Hello," he said. "Something I can do for you?"

"Are you Tomas Carranza?" the man asked bluntly.

"That's right. Oh, hell, you're not a process server, are you? I told Gustafson I'd pay that feed bill as soon as I can!"

"Oh no, I'm not here to serve you with a lawsuit, Mr. Carranza. But I *am* a lawyer." The man took a business card out of his shirt pocket and extended it.

Out of curiosity, Tommy took the card and glanced at it. The name J. Donald Lester was embossed on it in fancy black letters. The address was in Dallas.

"What's a Dallas lawyer doing all the way down here in the Valley?" Tommy asked with a frown.

"I represent a client in the area. Across the river in Cuidad Acuna, in fact."

Tommy grunted. "A Mexican with a Dallas lawyer. Must be a rich guy. What is he, a drug lord?"

"His name," J. Donald Lester said, "is Ernesto Diego Espinoza Ramirez."

Tommy went stiff and tight inside as he drew air sharply in through his nose. "*El Bruitre,*" he said in a hollow voice.

"Yes, yes, the Vulture," Lester said impatiently. "It's a very colorful name, but my client doesn't care for it, so why don't we just refer to him as Senor Ramirez?"

Tommy dropped the lawyer's card onto the concrete

of the parking lot. "Why don't we just call him a murdering, drug-running bastard and be done with it? And I think I'm done talking to you, too, Mr. Lester."

Tommy turned toward the front door of the pickup, but Lester stopped him with a hand on his arm. "Please, Mr. Carranza, I just want a few moments of your time."

Shaking off the lawyer's hand, Tommy said, "I don't talk to snakes, and if you work for Ramirez you're just as big a snake as he is, in my book."

"It's a matter of money," Lester said, raising his voice over the squeal of hinges as Tommy jerked the truck's door open. "A great deal of money."

A voice in the back of Tommy's head told him to get in the truck and drive away without paying any more attention to the gringo. But the mention of money piqued his interest. Not that he would ever take one red cent from Ramirez or his ilk. Any money they had would be indelibly stained with the blood and suffering of innocents.

Still, he was a naturally courteous man. And his youngest, Angelina, needed five thousand dollars' worth of orthodontic work to make her beautiful smile even more beautiful. That was what Julie said, anyway.

"I'll give you a minute," he said to Lester, "but I can tell you right now, I'm not gonna be interested in anything you have to say to me."

"Ten thousand dollars," Lester said.

Twice as much as what it would cost for Angelina's braces.

"What?" Tommy asked.

"Each month."

"You're offering to pay me ten grand a month!"

Lester nodded his sleekly barbered head. "That's correct."

"What for?"

"I think you know the answer to that, Mr. Carranza."

"Yeah," Tommy said. That brief moment of hope he'd had came crashing down. No way would anybody pay

that much money for something honest, especially not
Ramirez. "You want me to look the other way while the
Vulture's couriers bring that goddamn shit across my
land."

"It would be a perfectly legitimate arrangement, an
easement, if you will—"

"Easement this," Tommy said, and he brought up a
hard fist and smashed it into Lester's mouth.

He struck out of anger, furious that this sleazy Dallas
lawyer thought he could be bought off with drug money.
And he struck out of shame as well, because he hadn't
driven away without even listening to the bastard and because for a split second he had considered the offer. He
didn't know whom he was angrier with, himself or
Lester.

But it was the lawyer who got busted in the mouth. The
blow sent Lester staggering back across an empty parking
space. He slammed into another parked pickup. It had an
alarm installed and activated, and the siren began to blare
as Lester bounced off the driver's door and fell to the
pavement. He looked up at Tommy, stunned, with blood
on his mouth. His bruised lips began to swell.

"Lay down with dogs, get up with fleas, my daddy always
said," Tommy told him, raising his voice so he could be
heard over the yowling of the alarm. "Go back to Dallas,
Mr. Lawyer." The words were filled with contempt.

Lester couldn't get up. All he could do was glare bale-
fully as Tommy got in his pickup and drove away. Tommy
didn't look back.

Chapter 2

Stark knew Tommy Carranza well enough to recognize that something was on the younger man's mind when Stark visited the Carranza ranch that day. Tommy didn't seem to want to talk about it, though, so Stark didn't push it. A man didn't go sticking his nose in another fella's business without being asked to.

Tommy had just gotten back from Del Rio with a load of fence wire. Stark offered to help him stretch it in the places where his fences needed repair, but Tommy shook his head. "You've got your own work to do, John Howard. Besides, I've got Martin to help me."

Martin Carranza was Tommy's boy, twelve years old and turning into a good hand. With school out for the summer, Martin was doing a lot of work around the ranch.

Stark nodded. "All right, but if you need any help, you know where I am. What about that cow of yours and her calf?"

"If you don't mind keepin' 'em another night, I'll bring the trailer with me when we come over tomorrow and get them then."

"Sounds like a plan to me," Stark agreed.

"I'm sorry they strayed onto your range, John Howard."

A grin creased Stark's weathered face. "Don't worry

about that. Gettin' bogged down like it did, that old cow gave Uncle Newt an excuse to practice his roping."

Newton Stark was John Howard's uncle, brother to John Howard's daddy, Ethan. He had sold his half of the Diamond S to Ethan back when they both inherited the place from their father. To hear Newt tell it, he was a cowboy, and cowboys didn't have no place in their lives for sittin' in an office and doin' book work. Any chore that couldn't be done from the back of a horse wasn't worth doing, to Newt's way of thinking. Now in his eighties, he still lived on the Diamond S and did a fully day's work, blissfully ignorant of the business end of running a ranch.

"I thought you pulled that cow out of the sinkhole," Tommy commented.

"Well, Newt and me together got her loose," Stark said. "Anyway, her and the calf will be waiting for you tomorrow evening."

As Stark drove away in his pickup, he thought that he could just as easily have called Tommy and had this conversation by phone. Stark liked looking at a man when he talked to him, though. And he didn't mind overmuch the way Tommy's pretty wife, Julie, fussed over him and offered him lemonade when he visited. The lemonade had been cold and mighty good. Even though it wasn't quite noon yet, the heat of a Texas summer was in full force and the temperature was already around ninety-five. It would likely top out at 105 or 106 later that afternoon.

When Stark got back to the ranch he found a note from Elaine letting him know that she had gone into Del Rio to finish buying everything she would need for the Independence Day barbecue. She had left his lunch in the refrigerator since she would likely be gone most of the rest of the day. Stark got the bowl out and lifted the aluminum foil cover over it. Salad. He sighed. Elaine might have said she'd given up trying to get him to eat healthy, but she really hadn't.

Dutifully, he ate the rabbit food. Then he followed it with two thick peanut-butter-and-banana sandwiches he made himself.

With it being the Fourth of July and all, John Howard and Elaine had invited all their friends and neighbors. All the local ranchers from along the river and quite a few folks from town showed up at the sprawling, cottonwood-shaded ranch house on a small knoll that gave a view of the Rio Grande about a mile away. With help from Uncle Newt and Chaco Hernandez, one of the ranch hands who was Newt's best friend and companion, Stark had set up several picnic tables in the yard. Those tables were packed with food, some of it prepared by Elaine, some brought by the guests. Chaco, who was pushing seventy, was in charge of the barbecue pit, and wonderful smells filled the evening air.

It was hot, of course, because the sun was barely down and the air wouldn't cool off much for a while yet. But there was a good breeze and almost no humidity, so the weather was bearable. Stark had once seen a T-shirt with a picture on it of two sunbaked skeletons conversing. One of them was saying to the other, "But it's a *dry* heat." That was meant to be sarcastic, of course, but there was some truth to it. One time Stark had visited Houston and felt like he was fixin' to drown every time he took a deep breath of the humid air there. He hadn't been able to get out of that place fast enough. It was the armpit of Texas as far as he was concerned.

The ranchers naturally gravitated together while the women talked and the kids ran around yelling and play-ing. Stark found himself standing in a group of five of his friends: Tommy Carranza, of course, plus Devery Small, W.R. Smathers, Hubie Cornheiser, and Everett

Hatcher. The mood was glum despite the fact that this was supposed to be a celebration. All of the men had seen the newspaper and television reports about the latest outbreak of mad cow disease and knew what it would mean to their profits.

"It's not fair, damn it," Hubie said as they sipped from bottles of Lone Star beer. "Ain't never been a single mad cow found in Val Verde County. Every beef we raise is safe as it can be. But the buyers don't ever think about that."

W.R. nodded. "Prices are down across the board. That's what they always say, like it ain't their fault. And they claim they can't do a thing about it."

"They don't *want* to do anything about it," Stark said. "Naturally they want to pay as little as they can get by with."

"What they're gonna wind up doin' is starvin' us all out," Everett said. "Then they won't have to pay anything, so I reckon they'll be happy. But there won't be any beef no more, either."

Devery rubbed his jaw and said, "Yeah, beef prices are worrisome, all right, but to tell you the truth I'm more concerned about those damn drug smugglers."

Stark saw Tommy flick a startled glance toward Devery and ask, "What do you mean?"

Devery pointed toward the river with his beer bottle. "Hardly a night goes by when some o' that shit don't cross the range belonging to one or the other of us. You know, I really don't mind the illegals all that much, especially the ones who come across on their own. They're just tryin' to make a better life for themselves and their families, and I can almost respect that. But those drug runners ain't doin' anything except bringin' pure death across the river."

"I never have understood what would make a fella want to shoot that crap into his arm," W.R. said. "It just don't make no sense to me."

"The ones who do are too gutless to face up to life," Stark rumbled. "They'd rather run away, and they use the dope to do it."

"What's bad is that our daddies and our daddies' daddies and on back fought and died to tame this land," Devery went on. "They had to take on the Comanches and Mex bandidos—no offense, Tommy."

"None taken," Tommy said. "But there were Anglo bandits, too, you know."

Devery nodded. "Damn right, King Fisher and his like were every bit as bad, if not worse. Then you got your rattlesnakes and your scorpions, and the heat and the dust storms and everything else that those old boys had to put up with. But they beat all of it and made this valley a decent place to live. Now, though, it's bein' taken over by the same sort of bandidos who got run out of here a hundred years ago. They got cell phones and fancy guns and GPS systems now, but they're still bandidos as far as I'm concerned."

There were mutters of agreement from the men. Hubie said, "Looks to me like somebody ought to do something about all this."

"Who?" Devery shot back. "The government?"

"Government?" a harsh voice repeated. The men looked around to see that old Newton Stark, John Howard's uncle, had come up to join them, all six feet three inches of his cantankerous self. Newt continued. "All them fellas in Washington are a bunch o' black-suited, black-hearted bureaucratic robber barons, if you ask me. They ain't interested in helpin' anybody but their own selves."

"You don't think there are any good politicians?" W.R. asked.

Newt snorted. "I reckon there could be, but I ain't never seem 'em."

"It's not just the ones in Washington," Devery said. "There are plenty of 'em right here in Texas that I wouldn't trust as far as I could throw 'em. Like Norval Lee Hammond."

The sheriff of Val Verde County, Hammond was nearing the end of his second term in office. His first had been marked by controversy, but he had been reelected anyway, some said because of the campaign money that had poured into his coffers from unknown sources. Rumor had it those sources were heavily involved in the drug trade, but nothing had been proven. All anybody knew for sure was that arrests for drug trafficking weren't made very often, and when they were made, more of them were thrown out of court than seemed natural.

Stark and the others nodded in solemn agreement with Devery's comment about the sheriff. They might have gone on talking about the increased drug traffic across the border if Chaco hadn't called out that moment, "Barbecue's ready!"

Certain things go with barbecue. Nobody sits down to a big plate of brisket and arugala. But you've got your beans, your potato salad, your coleslaw and sliced onions and corn bread, and for dessert peach cobbler or apple cobbler or both, topped with homemade ice cream from a freezer with a hand-turned crank, not one of those electric jobs. Wash it all down with a cold bottle of beer or a big glass of iced tea with sweat dripping off it. That's eatin', son.

John Howard Stark was pleasantly full as he sat on one of the benches with his back to the picnic table and his long legs stretched out in front of him. He thought about unfastening his belt buckle and the button of his jeans, but he knew if he did that Elaine would notice and likely swat him one on the back of the head. Country music played from the portable stereo he'd set up earlier, and a few couples were dancing as

George Strait sang about getting to Amarillo by morning. Stark sipped his beer, content.

He watched Tommy Carranza dancing with Julie. Tommy was handsome enough in a rough-hewn way, but Julie was really a beauty, taut and tanned with hair as black as a raven's wing hanging straight down her back. Her high cheekbones and piercing dark eyes bespoke her Indian blood.

Elaine sat down beside Stark and said, "What are you doing?"

"Thinking about how pretty Julie Carranza is."

She punched him lightly on the arm. "What kind of a man says something like that to his wife?"

"The honest kind?"

"Well, if you want to put it that way . . . and she is awfully pretty."

"You know you don't have anything to be jealous about. I never said she was prettier than you. Nobody is."

"Thank you, John Howard. You never were a man with a smooth line of talk, but you say what you mean and mean what you say, and a woman appreciates that. This one does, anyway."

Stark put his arm around her shoulders and she rested her head against him. They sat there like that for several minutes, happy to be with each other and to be surrounded by their friends. At moments like this, all thoughts of trouble went away.

The problem was that moments like that never lasted long enough. In this case, the song ended, the dancing stopped, and Tommy and Julie came over to the bench where Stark sat with Elaine.

"John Howard, I need to talk to you for a minute," Tommy said.

"Uh-oh, I know that tone," Julie said. "Something's wrong, isn't it?"

Tommy shook his head. "Of course not. I just need to talk a little business with John Howard here."

"Man talk, he means," Elaine said as she stood up. "You'd think they'd know by now that it's the twenty-first century and such chauvinistic attitudes are totally outdated."

"They're a couple of throwbacks," Julie said, but she was grinning as she said it.

Stark got to his feet, too, and jerked a thumb toward the barn. "Come on, Tommy, let's go get that cow and her calf and load 'em up. That'll give us a chance to talk in peace."

As they started toward the barn, Tommy asked quietly, "Elaine wasn't really upset, was she?"

"Naw, she was just hoo-rawin', us. She's feisty that way."

Tommy changed the subject by asking, "You hear anything from the boys lately?"

"Got e-mail from both of 'em a couple of days ago. They say they're doing fine, but they don't know when they'll be back from over there."

Both of John Howard and Elaine's sons were in the military. The older boy, David, was in the navy, a pilot flying off an aircraft carrier somewhere in the Middle East. Stark didn't know where, exactly. They younger one, Peter, was a lieutenant colonel in the marines, a leatherneck like his old man, and he'd been pulling a tour of duty in Iraq for the past year.

"You must worry about them being in harm's way," Tommy said.

Stark grunted. "This day and age, with all the evil loose in the world, every American is in harm's way no matter where he is or what he's doing. I reckon we're safer here than the boys are where they are, but at least they've got the weapons to fight back. Over here we're supposed to just roll over and take whatever's dished out to us, no matter how bad it is. Otherwise we ain't bein' sensitive enough to other folks' beliefs and cultures." He shook his head. "Just once I'd like to see other folks give a little respect to *our* beliefs and culture."

"Roger that," Tommy said.

Stark stopped, and the younger man did likewise. They were in a patch of shadow, and even though Stark couldn't see Tommy's face all that clearly, he looked at him head-on and said, "You didn't ask to talk just to hear me rant about such things. Something's bothering you, Tommy. What is it?"

"You can tell?"

"Hell, I've known you for over thirty years. Of course I can tell." Stark made a shrewd guess. "It's something about all the drug smuggling that's been goin' on. I saw the way you reacted when Devery brought it up."

Tommy shifted his feet uneasily. "When I was in Del Rio yesterday picking up those rolls of fence, a guy talked to me."

"What guy?"

"A lawyer from Dallas. He gave me his card. His name was J. Donald Lester."

"I never did really trust a man who uses his first initial and middle name like that. Seems like he's puttin' on airs. What did ol' J. Donald want?"

"I won't beat around the bush, John Howard. He works for the Vulture, and he wanted to pay me ten grand a month to look the other way while Ramirez's couriers bring drugs across my land."

Stark let out a low whistle. "The Vulture, eh? That ain't good. What did you do?"

"I'm ashamed to say I thought about it. I wouldn't admit that to anybody else, John Howard, not even to Julie."

"Thought about it for how long?" Stark asked grimly.

"About half a second."

"And then?"

"And then I busted him a good one in the mouth."

Stark couldn't hold back an explosive bark of laughter. "Good for you. I knew you wouldn't ever go for any sort of deal like that."

"Well, I'm glad you know that, because like I said, for a minute there I considered it. And it's been eatin' me up ever since."

Stark put a hand on his friend's shoulder. "No need for that. You did the right thing."

"Did I? I'm not so sure."

"You mean you think you should have taken the deal?"

"No, of course not. But doing what I did . . . it's bound to make an enemy out of Ramirez."

Stark rubbed his jaw, feeling the calluses on his fingertips scrape against the bristles of his beard. "Yeah, there is that. I didn't think about it at first."

"Neither did I. But now I wonder if I've put my family in danger."

One thing was sure, thought Stark. The Vulture was a bad man to cross. Just about the baddest man possible. . . .